His Love

La Petite Mort Club Intimate Encounters

Ellis O. Day

Cover design by Teragram Author Services

I love to hear from readers so email me at
authorellisoday@gmail.com

https://www.EllisODay.com

Follow me

Facebook
https://www.facebook.com/EllisODayRomanceAuthor/

Closed FB Group (sneak peeks, sample chapters, and other bonuses)
https://www.facebook.com/groups/153238782143373

Bookbub
https://www.bookbub.com/authors/ellis-o-day

Amazon
https://www.amazon.com/Ellis-O-Day/e/B072QL6B3G/ref=dp_byline_cont_ebooks_1

Instagram
https://www.instagram.com/authorellisoday/

Join My Readers' Group and for a limited time get the entire Six Nights of Sin series for FREE

(THERE'S A PEEK OF BOOK ONE AT THE END OF THIS BOOK)

Click Here to Get Your FREE Books

Here's What You Get When You

Join My Readers' Group

Win Before You Can Buy
Exclusive Giveaways
Free Books
Sneak Peeks

Ellis O. Day

CHAPTER 1: TERRY

Terry sat on the couch in the living room of their private suite at La Petite Mort Club while Maggie finished her bath. Last night, their first night here as a couple, he'd lost control of the scene. He shouldn't have. He knew better but his feelings for Maggie were so raw that he'd lost his head. Lucky for him, she was fine with everything they'd done.

His dick twitched in his pants at the memory. She'd been so hot, hanging from the ceiling, wet and waiting for him, eager for him. He ran his hand through his still damp hair. He'd just fucked her in the tub and he wanted her again. She drove him wild and he loved it. That word plowed from his head to his heart, sending ice through his veins and making his dick duck and run for cover. He'd fallen in love with her. Him. The man who'd sworn to never, ever let that happen again, had succumbed. He stood and walked to the bar. It was only late morning but this called for a shot.

He poured two fingers of Glenlivet in a glass and tossed it back, sighing as the burn chased away some of the ice in his blood. This wouldn't be like the last time. Unlike his ex, Maggie definitely liked men. She enjoyed sex as much as he did. Plus, she loved him. She'd been telling him so for months now.

He stared at his empty glass, his heart twisting. It must kill her when he didn't say it back. He was a fucking coward. He had to tell her. He would tell her but it had to be perfect—the perfect time and the perfect place. He'd only realized that he loved her yesterday, right before she'd told him about his surprise weekend at the Club. If he told her now, she might think he was only saying it because she'd come to the Club with him.

Her self-esteem was shaky due to her fuckhead of an ex-husband. He needed her to know that he loved her no matter what. That this was forever for him. It'd better be forever for her too. He poured another shot and gulped it down. He couldn't lose her. He hit his forehead against the cabinet several times. Fuck, how had he let this happen? He didn't want to love her, to be vulnerable like that but he couldn't go back to not having her or her kids in his life. He had to tell her how he felt but not now and definitely not here. He took a deep breath, stuffing the panic back down into his gut.

He'd tell her later this week. After they picked up the kids from Nick and Sarah's house on Sunday, they'd spend the rest of their vacation in paradise. He'd plan the entire day—beach, picnic, games with the kids and a movie. Later, after the children were in bed, he'd tell her how he felt and then show her by making love to her, letting her feel his heart with every touch.

A knock sounded and he glanced at his watch. Damn. The masseuse was already here. He strolled to the door and opened it.

"Hi, I'm Kevin and I'm here for the couples massage." The guy was in his late twenties or early thirties and good looking with sandy blonde hair, brown eyes and an easy smile.

"I'm Terry." He shook the guy's hand and then stepped aside. "You can set up in the living room."

Kevin nodded, carrying the masseuse table and bag over by the couch.

"I'll go get Maggie." He strode to the bathroom, his dick already starting to wake. Today and tonight, he'd push her limits with kink, but nothing would make him lose control again—no matter how hot she was or how sexy. He was keeping his cool.

CHAPTER 2: MAGGIE

Maggie let the heat from the bath water soak into her muscles, washing away the soreness. Yesterday had been wild—wonderful but wild. Her butt still stung and she was tender from the lash on her thighs and Terry's dick between them. Sometimes he liked it rough and so did she. She loved the way he filled her, his cock big and hard stretching her and bringing her an almost unbearable pleasure, but she paid the next day.

These hot baths helped, thank God, because there was no reprieve from his sexual appetites. If the man wanted food as much as sex, he'd weigh a thousand pounds. She grinned as she ran the loofa up her arm and over her breast. The scrape across her nipple ignited the embers in her blood that Terry had assuaged earlier when he'd joined her in the tub. He was insatiable and she'd never felt so wanted as when she was with him. He showed it every day by helping with the kids, giving her silly little presents and his desire. He made it clear that he cared for her. She frowned, dragging the loofa up her other arm. She hated that word. Care. It wasn't enough but it might be all she got.

"If you're not doing it right, I'll be happy to help." Terry's deep voice made her drop the loofa.

Instinctively she covered her breasts but that only lasted a second. Her hands fell away, searching the water for the sponge. He liked to look at her and she liked how his gaze darkened, feeling almost like a caress on her skin. "When did you come in?"

"A moment ago. Long enough to see you frowning." He grabbed a towel and walked to the tub, his dark eyes roaming over her naked body. "Is your head hurting again? Do you need me to get you some more Tylenol?"

"No. Everything's fine." Emotion clogged her throat. He was so caring but did he love her?

He raised his brow. "You frown when you're happy now?" He opened the towel and held it out for her.

The man was as tenacious as he was stubborn. She should've gone with the headache excuse. Since she hadn't, she needed to change the topic before he forced her to lie to him. She was not ruining their weekend because she was being emotional and foolish. "You've been quiet today."

He'd been almost stoic. Several times she'd caught him staring at her only to look away when she glanced in his direction. It wasn't like him to be evasive and he certainly wasn't shy.

"Have I?" His eyes were locked on her breasts as he offered her his hand.

"Yes." She took it as she stepped out of the tub.

"Perhaps, it only seems like that since there are no children around filling every second with chatter." He wrapped the towel around her and began rubbing her dry, the soft cloth rough on her sensitive skin.

"Maybe." She wasn't buying it. They had every other weekend alone when the kids went to their father's house. She didn't want to but she had to ask...again. "You sure you're not—"

He grabbed the heart shape ring affixed to her collar and tugged her to him. "For the last time, I am not upset about last night. I was in charge. Your actions were my decision. My responsibility."

"Are you sure?" She rested her hand on his chest, her body pressing against his. "You seem upset today."

He pulled her up by the collar until she was on tiptoe. "I'm sure. I just have a lot on my mind."

"Like what?" She searched his eyes. He was hiding something.

"Like, last night was fucking hot and I'm going to make sure that today and tonight are even hotter."

She almost melted right there on the floor. She wasn't sure if she was ready for another scene like last night and yet her body ached for it.

"Now, go into the living room before we miss our couples massage."

"Oh, they're here already?"

"Yep." He pulled her against him. His dick, hard and

ready, pressed into her belly. "And if you don't move, I'm going to fuck you in the bathroom again, but this time, I'm bending you over the tub." He stepped away from her.

"That sounds lovely." She let the towel drop and moved closer to him. She didn't need a massage. She needed him.

"Later." He almost growled. "Right now, the massage."

"Fine." She frowned before she bent, wiggling her hips as she grabbed the towel.

"Rabbit, you're asking for it." He swatted her ass.

"And I'd love for you to *give it* to me, Sir." She straightened.

"Go." He gave her a gentle push toward the door. "I have everything planned. No matter how tempting you are, I'm not going to deviate from our schedule."

"Okay. Okay, but a rabbit can try." She grinned as she strolled out of the room, letting her hips sway seductively.

A guy in all black with blonde hair and a sexy smile stood near a table. "Hi, I'm Kevin. I'll be your masseuse today."

"Ah…where's the other masseuse?"

"It's just me," said Kevin.

Terry walked up behind her, the heat from his body sinking into her skin.

"Come on. Hop on up." Kevin patted the table.

It was covered in a white fitted sheet. Where was the other sheet? The one that went over the person being massaged.

"Are you going to massage both of us?" She glanced at Terry and the heat in his dark eyes caused wetness to pool between her legs. She knew that look. Her body knew that look; it meant pleasure. Her blood slowed in her veins, flowing thick and sweet like honey. "I thought this was a couples massage."

"It is. La Petite Mort Club style." His grin widened. "Now, get on the table like a good Sub."

CHAPTER 3: MAGGIE

"May I call you Maggie?" Kevin smiled, nothing but friendly professionalism on his face.

"Yes, of course." Maggie glanced at the table. Where was that sheet?

"Great. Then let's get started," said Kevin. "Are there any areas you want me to focus on? Any place you're having pain or tension?"

"Ah...no."

"No place that's sore at all?" The pure innocence in Terry's voice contrasted with the smirk on his handsome face as he walked to the couch and sat.

She made a face at him and his grin widened. He could be such an ass.

"Maggie, you have to tell me where you hurt if you want me to help." Kevin winked at her. "Don't worry. I've worked here a long time."

"Well, I am a little sore"—her face heated—"on my lower back."

"Your lower back? Really? That's where you're sore?"

Terry's dark eyes danced with humor.

Lord, he could be a jerk sometimes. "Okay. A bit lower than that." She touched her hip.

"Ah. The gluteus maximus area." Kevin grinned. "We get that a lot around here."

Terry barked out a laugh. "I bet you do."

"I have some oil that'll make you feel as good as new." Kevin pulled a bottle from his bag and hooked it to his belt.

"Oh...ah..." She glanced at Terry but he didn't seem the least bit concerned that this good looking, younger man was going to rub her ass.

"Shall we start." Kevin stared at her expectantly.

"Uhm..." The masseuse wasn't leaving. The other massage therapists had always left the room when she'd undressed but she had a feeling this wasn't going to be anything at all like her previous massages.

"Drop the towel, rabbit." Terry's voice had grown husky and his eyes now sparkled with desire.

She hesitated. She wasn't sure why. Last night she'd been naked and then some in front of several men, but this was daytime. She and Terry hadn't been fooling around. She wasn't horny. The pulse beating between her legs called her on her lie. Okay. This was turning her on but...

"Would you like for me to turn around?" asked Kevin.

"No," said Terry.

She shot him a dirty look. She would've liked that.

"Think about this, rabbit." Terry stood and walked over to her. "He's going to see you naked on the table.

10

Massage your body. Touch you."

"But only in the..." She hesitated, not sure how to finish that sentence. She'd been going to say "right places" but she could imagine Terry's response to that.

"Only where, rabbit?" He leaned down by her ear. "Where do you want Kevin to touch you?"

She swallowed. "I just want a massage. A regular one." She felt his grin against the side of her head.

"You'll like this one better. I promise."

She turned, her lips a breath from his. She trusted him and he didn't like to share. "Okay." She dropped the towel.

His gaze traveled down her body, his face hardening with desire and causing a chain reaction in her. Her pussy pulsed strong and needy, empty but yearning to be touched, kissed, filled.

"Good, rabbit. Now, get on the table so Kevin can give you that massage."

CHAPTER 4: TERRY

Terry held back his smile as Maggie climbed onto the table, eyes darting everywhere except at Kevin. She stretched out, placing her face in the crescent headrest.

"Do you like it soft, firm or hard?" Kevin's eyes sparkled with humor.

"Excuse me?" Maggie started to sit up and then glanced down at her luscious breasts and dropped back onto the table.

"The pressure," said Kevin.

"Oh," she squeaked. "Medium I guess."

"Perfect." Kevin squirted oil in his hands and ran them down Maggie's back in a long stroke that forced him to lean over her head.

"What did you think he meant, rabbit?" Terry settled back against the couch, ready to enjoy the show.

"Ah." She lifted her head, her eyes meeting Kevin's crotch and her face turning bright red before she dropped onto the headrest.

"Tsk, tsk. What a dirty mind you have, rabbit."

"And whose fault is that?" she mumbled.

He laughed. "You're welcome."

"You need to relax." Kevin continued to work the muscles along her back.

"Sorry."

"Why don't you put on that music you guys use?" Terry wanted her good and relaxed for later.

"Great idea." Kevin walked to the couch and grabbed his phone and a speaker from his bag. Soon, the sound of rain filled the room. "Now, let's get you relaxed." He returned to the table, his strong hands pressing down on her back, his fingers searching for the knots and gently working out the kinks.

Terry's eyes roamed over her lush, naked frame, his dick swelling in anticipation. She'd be soft and sleepy and so relaxed that he'd be able to slide right inside her and make her come.

Kevin moved along her back and arms, working her muscles, but Maggie wasn't relaxing. She twitched every time his hands got near her butt.

"Relax, Maggie," said Terry.

"I'm trying."

"But..." He waited.

"It's hard with you watching." She leaned up a little. "I'm sorry."

"Don't be. Just let your mind wander. Pretend I'm not here."

She snorted as she put her head back in the headrest.

"I'll try but that's not going to be possible."

His chest puffed up with pride. Good. She couldn't ignore him or forget about him. She knew what he wanted. What he always wanted—her. Seeing her lying there, naked except for the collar proclaiming she was his while Kevin massaged that satiny flesh made him want nothing more than to join the masseuse and explore the soft, dark spaces that'd make her purr.

The downside to her awareness was that she should be able to relax around him. He was her Dom. He'd care for her and protect her above all else.

Kevin glanced at him, shaking his head. This wasn't working.

"You're not relaxing." He stood and Maggie lifted her head slightly.

"Sorry."

"Hmm." He strode into the bedroom and came back with a sheet, draping it over her ass. "Maybe this will help."

"Yes, it does. Thank you." She smiled at him, warm and filled with love.

His knees almost buckled. She was so fucking appreciative of every little thing he did for her it humbled him and made him want to beat her ex into a bloody pulp. The man had abused her giving nature but he knew what a true gift it was. "Of course. I'd do anything for you, even deny myself."

"Deny yourself?"

"Yes, watching you get a massage."

"You're enjoying this?"

He dipped his head to her ear. "I could grab your hand and show you exactly how much."

She turned so her lips were near his. "Really? This is turning you on?"

"Very much." He knew exactly what was coming next but she should have some idea where this was headed. They'd been together long enough.

"Oh." Her cheeks heated. "You can remove the sheet."

"No. I want you to relax." He kissed her gently.

"But—"

"You come first. Always. At least once but preferably several times before I get my turn."

"Terry." Her face heated as her eyes darted to Kevin.

He laughed and took a step back. "You know, I don't think the sheet is enough. Isn't the room usually dark too?"

"Yes," said Kevin. "But those rooms have small lights so that I can see. If I make this room dark, I'll be fumbling around in here." He skimmed his finger down her spine, stopping where it joined her hip bone. "You wouldn't want me accidentally massaging someplace you don't want me to touch, would you?" He winked at Terry.

"No. I'll shut my eyes. It'll be fine."

"I don't think that's good enough. You could've shut your eyes earlier." Terry snapped his fingers. "I got it. One minute." He went into the bedroom and came back with a blindfold. "I think this will work perfectly."

Terry grinned as Maggie's eyes widened.

CHAPTER 5: MAGGIE

Maggie tried to relax as Kevin's strong fingers rubbed along her muscles. He was good at his job, really good and professional. He never once dipped beneath the sheet that covered her butt. His hands felt wonderful but even though she was blindfolded, she swore she could feel Terry's dark gaze on her skin.

"This isn't working." Kevin sighed and stepped back. "She's as tense as if she were getting arrested."

"I'm sorry. I'm trying." She leaned up, reaching for the blindfold.

The couch creaked as Terry stood and grabbed her wrist. "Keep it on, rabbit."

"Yes, Sir." She lowered back to the table.

"Maybe you'd be more comfortable if I helped. Kevin, give me some oil."

Terry touching her would make her the opposite of relaxed. "Ah...Ter...Sir, I don't think..."

"Perfect. Don't think. Just feel."

"But…" She leaned up.

Terry's hand pressed on her upper back as he kissed her cheek. "Just relax and enjoy your massage. I have a busy night planned for us." His mouth came down on her shoulder, kissing up to her neck, his lips stopping at her ear. "Trust me. You want to save your energy."

She shivered at his wicked promise. He'd been very closed mouthed about tonight, just saying that it'd be only her and him. Before Terry, she'd never imagined all the positions and toys that a couple could use to enhance love making. The sex itself would've been enough. Terry was a fabulous lover—attentive, rough, tender, playful. Every time it was different and the same—wonderful. He knew her and her body better than she did.

His large hand ran across her ass, squeezing gently. "How's that feel?"

"Ah…" *Too good.* Her muscles clenched around the butt plug and she shivered again.

"Hmm. Should probably remove this." His fingers slid between her cheeks.

"Terry…not with…" She gasped as he pulled the toy from her.

"Don't be embarrassed. I'm sure Kevin has seen his share of these."

"Yep." Kevin's fingers continued to work along her spine. "I'd be more surprised not seeing one."

"Now, relax, rabbit and enjoy." Terry's thumbs worked the tension from her butt cheeks.

She stifled a groan as his hands cupped her ass and then

massaged the muscles along her lower back. Another pair of strong hands stroked along her shoulders, working out the kinks. It was glorious. She sighed as Terry and Kevin's hands slid along her body.

One of them moved to her arms, rubbing up and down, pushing the tension to her hands and then working it out through her fingers. Her mind drifted to nothing but waves of pleasure—but not the hot, wicked kind Terry invoked, but the slow contentment that came before sleep.

CHAPTER 6: TERRY

Terry ran his hands along the smooth skin of Maggie's back. She was so fucking soft and warm, so trusting. He couldn't get enough of her.

"I think this is a first." Kevin's voice was low as he wiped his hands on a towel.

"Yeah." No other woman he knew would've fallen asleep while getting massaged by her lover and a stranger at La Petite Mort Club. Her trust made his heart wrench inside his chest. He'd never betray her or hurt her. Never.

Kevin turned off the music and began gathering his things.

"Leave the oil that takes away the sting." Terry forced himself to stop touching Maggie and cleaned his hands with a towel before grabbing his wallet.

"Sure." Kevin dug in the bag and put one of the vials on the table by the couch.

"Thanks. I'm having a crew…" He glanced at Maggie. He was pretty sure she was sleeping but she could be devious in her curiosity. She'd been pestering him all day about his plans for the night. He walked to the door and Kevin followed. "I'll have them grab your table when they set up the Mobile Saint."

"Perfect. Tell them to leave it in the supply room. I'll pick it up later."

"Thanks." He handed Kevin a stack of bills before he closed the door and leaned against it.

His goddess hadn't moved. His little rabbit with ruffled hair and a lush body slick with oil really was sound asleep. His dick, which had been hard since before the massage, started to protest its confinement. She was right there, naked except for his collar around her neck. Fuck. That was the wrong thing to think about. His dick wasn't relaxing and why should it. She wouldn't mind him waking her for sex. He did it all the time.

He strode toward her, grabbing the oil. She'd really enjoyed it when Kevin had rubbed it on her muscles. He should put some more on her. He was her Dom. Her comfort came before his and he didn't want her sore for tonight. He tugged at his pants, trying to give his erection some room but that eager appendage only grew more. He opened the bottle of oil but paused when she sighed. He put the container down and ran his hand down her arm to her hand. He'd never tire of touching her, but he could wait. She needed her sleep. Last night was long and tonight would be longer. The least he could do was let her get some rest because later he'd take her to another level of pleasure and desire.

CHAPTER 7: TERRY

Terry glanced at the time on his laptop. Maggie had been sleeping for over an hour. He closed the computer and put it aside as he got out of bed.

After the masseuse had left, he'd gone to the bedroom, hoping to take a nap but that hadn't worked, not with his cock focused on the naked woman in the other room. So, he'd worked—the best he could with his eyes constantly drifting to the door and his mind trying to convince him to check on her to ensure that she was warm and comfortable. Right. If he'd gone back into that room, he'd have fucked her.

He walked into the kitchen and grabbed a bottle of water before letting his eyes wander to Maggie. The sheet was still draped across her lower back and butt but it looked a bit rumpled. His gaze landed on the oil. She may need some more. They had time before he had to have her out of here so the team could set up the Mobile Saint. He took a large gulp of water as he headed across the room.

At some point, she'd shifted downward, removing her

face from the headrest and exposing her cheek and lips. She was temptation incarnate for a man like him. Innocence and sin wrapped up in a delicious naked package. Her cheek was slightly flushed and her pink lips open a little as she slept— innocent, trusting. That image contrasted sharply with the mask covering her eyes, her oil slick nakedness and her hair. Fuck, that hair called to him. It was wanton and wild, the curls tumbling all around and cascading down her side.

He ran his hand over her cheek, moving her hair and bending to kiss her. He froze, except for his dick which rose even more. He'd forgotten about the collar. Lust roared through him. She was his. Always. Fuck, he loved her so much he could barely breathe. Sleeping or not, he had to touch her.

CHAPTER 8: MAGGIE

"Sorry. I think I dozed off." Maggie slowly woke as strong hands continued to massage her muscles. She was warm and relaxed. It was heaven.

The hands moved to her shoulders and she sighed. It felt wonderful. Her body was like living mercury, fluid and yet formed. His hands worked their way down her spine, skimming along the sheet before slipping underneath. Her breath caught as he cupped her ass.

"Terry?" It had to be him.

"Shhh." He moved his hands lower.

In her half-asleep state she hadn't noticed that there was only one set of hands on her. Was Terry watching again? That's what he'd wanted to do.

His hands left for a moment and then came back, slicker than before. They ran up and down her calf, soothing her muscles. She sank into the mattress. If Terry wanted to watch, let him. This man's hands were magic. Long, strong strokes followed by more oil and then more pressure, working their way up her leg.

She stiffened as he spread her legs a little wider. "Terry, that's you, right?"

"Shhh." He pushed the sheet up to her waist.

"Ah…" She squeaked as he nipped her ass. "Hold on a minute."

Terry's rich chuckle filled the room and then lips, warm and familiar met hers. "Relax. It's me."

"Oh, you jerk." She pulled off the blindfold. They were alone. All the masseuse's things besides the table were gone.

"You fell asleep." He brushed the hair from her face. "I was going to let you sleep longer but…" He hooked his finger in her collar. "When I saw this"—his eyes searched hers and there was something rich and promising in his gaze—"I had to touch you."

She ran her hand over his face, loving the feel of his whiskers. The man had to shave at least twice a day to keep them at bay. "You can wake me with touches or kisses anytime."

His mouth dipped down to hers, his tongue sliding inside to explore a long moment before he parted. "Now, lay back down, rabbit and let me finish your massage."

"Yes, Sir." She dropped onto the table, no longer the least bit relaxed and that was perfect because Terry knew how to make her boneless better than anyone–even a trained masseuse with the hands of a magician.

CHAPTER 9: TERRY

Terry massaged Maggie's back, content for the moment to give her nothing more than comfort with his touch. His hands glided along her soft skin, the oil making it even smoother than normal.

Kevin had worked out the little knots of tension, so all that was left was supple, relaxed muscles. He lengthened his strokes, unable to stay away from those places that called to him. His hand skimmed over her ass. "How does this feel?"

"Wonderful." She almost melted into the table.

"Not still sore from last night?" His hand stroked across her outer thigh.

"No. The oil really helped."

"Good." He bent, kissing along where her back met her butt. "I'll go easy tonight."

"You don't have to." She turned, watching him.

"I'll never hurt you more than you'll enjoy or push you further than you want to go." He kissed her fingers and her palm. His lips lingering on her ring finger. It was empty. It shouldn't be. His mouth froze and he cleared his throat before putting her hand back down on the mattress. That thought needed to go the fuck away. He was not getting married again. Ever.

"I know."

He straightened, staring at her. There was no way he'd said that out loud.

"I trust you and my butt and legs don't hurt anymore. So, if you want to…" Her cheeks heated slightly.

Thank God. He hadn't said it out loud. His thoughts on marriage weren't a secret. They'd talked about it before but there was no reason for him to repeat it, especially at a time like this.

"Tonight. This entire weekend. Whatever you want," she said.

With those three little words, all thoughts except fucking her fled. He grabbed her hair, wrapping it around his fist and pulling up her head as he leaned down to her ear. "You have to stop saying that."

"But I mean it." Her hazel eyes were filled with trust and desire.

He groaned against her neck, stifling his words of love. If he said them now, she'd think it was because of sex but that was only a tiny part of why he loved her. "Rabbit, you're tempting me."

"Happy birthday, Terry. Whatever you want. All weekend long." Her words were a challenge he couldn't refuse.

"As you wish." He nipped her ear. Innocent massage was done. It was time to play.

CHAPTER 10: MAGGIE

Maggie's entire body tingled and not just because Terry nipped her ear. His hands ran down her back in a long caress that felt wonderful. He stroked over her butt, pressing firmly on the cheeks before his fingers traipsed along her crack. Her breath stilled but he didn't wander into forbidden territory. Instead, his caress moved down her rear to the outer part of her thighs as if he were intent on obeying the masseuse handbook, if there was such a thing. Deep down, she knew this massage was going to have a happy ending but her body, still lethargic, wasn't paying attention. Soon her thoughts faded, drifting along with the feel of his hands. He worked the muscles in her calf, moving to her thigh. His hands slid up her leg and down, his long fingers easing her muscles, and then repeating the motion but this time his caress went farther up her leg. He continued to move in strong fluid strokes but each one brought him closer and closer to the juncture between her thighs.

Her body, once sleepy, was wide awake and tense, her

pussy throbbing in anticipation of his touch. His hands returned, pressing firmly along her muscles, the tips of his fingers brushing the outer lips of her pussy. She shifted a little, opening her legs to give him room to play.

He chuckled softly.

The ass. She closed her legs, but his hands gripped her thighs.

"No take-backs."

"No take-back doesn't count if someone laughs at the gift."

"I didn't laugh." He spread her legs farther.

"I heard you. It wasn't a full-blown laugh but—"

"Nope." His breath was hot on the back of her leg. "Didn't happen."

Her body tensed. His fingers would be nice but his lips...and tongue...that'd be exquisite.

"I'd never"—he let his mouth brush against her thigh, traveling inward and upward with each word—"laugh at your eagerness to be fucked." He shoved her legs farther apart, his breath tickling her pussy.

She wanted to beg, to plead for him to touch her but... "You've laughed at me dozens of times."

"You're mistaken." He smiled, letting her feel it against her skin.

"I am not." She really should let this go. "You do it all the time."

"Do what?" He blew on her pussy and she shivered.

"Make me want you."

"That I'll admit to." His tongue darted out, a quick lick along her folds.

"Oh…god…yes." She needed his mouth on her.

"But I'd never laugh at you." He grabbed her ass and spread her cheeks.

"You just did."

"My rabbit's being stubborn today."

"My Sir is lying." That should stop him. He prided himself on his brutal honesty.

"I'm not lying." He grabbed her and rolled her onto her back. "I don't lie." His dark eyes were hot with passion and a spark of anger.

She wanted him even more. "Then admit you laughed." She arched her back, offering her breasts to him in a silent plea.

"I did not"—he bent until his face was next to hers—"laugh. I'd never laugh at you. I lo…" He clamped his mouth shut. "I'd never laugh at you," he repeated.

Her heart soared. He'd been going to say something else. Had it been that he loved her? She wanted to wrap her arms and legs around him and beg him to finish what he'd been going to say but pushing him always ended with them fighting. The only time he was okay with it was when they played. So, she'd play. "Then what do you call that snort of laughter?"

"Amusement." He ran his hand along her cheek and kissed her gently. "But never laughter."

"Same thing."

"No, there's a big difference." He grabbed her hips and

pulled her down to the edge of the table so her pussy cradled his erection. "Yes, your eagerness for my dick makes me happy." Her rocked against her. "Very, very happy and it amuses me when you try and prod me to move faster"—he kissed her neck—"because, I want nothing more than to push inside you and fuck you until we both come."

"Then why don't you?"

His gaze was so hot it almost burnt her. "Because we'll both enjoy it so much more if I make you wait. Make me wait."

"You sure?" She put her feet on the table and lifted, rubbing against his cock. Her eyes drifted closed as his hardness both eased and inflamed her ache. She needed him now.

"Yes." He rested his forehead on hers, his hips rocking against her. "Fuck…Maggie."

His words were a warning growl but she didn't care. She reached between them, running her hands along his dick. Poor thing was still trapped in his pants. "I don't think you are"—she squeezed him—"sure you want to wait."

"Rabbit, don't push it." His desperate, gravelly voice sent tingles racing through her.

"But I want to." She was done playing. She wanted him inside her. She squeezed him tighter, stroking along his length while her other hand unbuttoned his pants. She slid the zipper down until she could reach inside and grasp his heat. "So, Sir what are you going to do about it?"

CHAPTER 11: TERRY

That was it. Terry's control snapped. He shoved down his pants and grabbed Maggie's thighs pulling her almost off the table.

"Terry…" She squeaked, her hand coming off his dick to grab his arm.

He was beyond words. The only thought in his head was getting inside her. He'd waited and watched while she'd lain naked, another man touching her soft skin, and then he'd had his turn to explore. Now, he had to own it. Make her quiver in need for him. Feel her clasp around him, tugging him deeper inside her body until he exploded.

He grabbed his dick, positioning himself at her entrance. He inhaled at the feel of her wet heat, eager for him. His fingers dug into her hips. "Look at me." He had to see her eyes, see what she felt when he entered her.

Her gaze locked with his, her hazel eyes dark green with desire. He couldn't wait another minute. He pushed inside, in one hard thrust. Her eyes widened and her lips parted on a gasp that went straight to his balls, making them tighten. His hips rocked, his dick moving in and out but not far. He was past playing, past desiring the feel of the first slide into her slick heat. He needed her around him always. Tight and hot. Her wet, eager pussy clasping him and keeping him close. His thrusts came faster and harder, his fingers digging into the soft flesh of her ass. Her breasts swayed with his motion. He needed to feel them, feel her surround him. He slid his finger through the heart shaped O-ring on her collar and tugged. "Come here."

She sat up, moaning as her movement caused his cock to shift inside her. He captured the sound with his lips, his tongue diving into her mouth as his dick drove into her body. He grabbed her neck, holding her for his assault. Her arms wrapped around him and her breasts pressed against his chest, her hard, little nipples rubbing against him.

"Fuck, Maggie." He was close. He should slow down but he didn't want to wait. He'd take his time tonight. He'd spend hours teasing her and making her come. He'd play until she begged him to stop. He'd wring every last orgasm from her body, but right now was for him.

"Terry…" Her fingers dug into his biceps as she buried her face in his neck.

She was close too but not as close as him. He grabbed her thighs, lifting her legs and angling her ass as he pumped into her. She moaned long and loud in his ear. He'd found the spot. The one that drove her fucking insane. He increased his pace, his dick rubbing against that spongy paradise and making her body clamp around him so tight he bit his lip to keep from exploding. He bent, his mouth latching onto her nipple sucking hard and she screamed, her body bucking against his, squeezing him and pulling him over the edge with her.

CHAPTER 12: MAGGIE

Maggie stared at herself in the bathroom mirror. A ponytail just didn't work with this dress, no matter how much Terry liked that hairstyle. Her cheeks heated at the memory, his fist in her hair while they made love. *Was that what he was doing? She was making love, but was he?* She pushed that thought aside. She wasn't going to let her insecurities ruin this weekend or her life with Terry. He wasn't the kind of man to use words like love. Instead, he showed her with his actions and his gifts. Her fingers drifted over her collar. It was lovely and expensive but mostly she liked it because it made his dark eyes almost glow when he looked at her.

He was a possessive man and as much as the modern, independent woman she was should scoff at it, her genetics wouldn't let her. She liked being his as much as she liked him being hers. She was possessive too.

"Maggie, hurry up. I'm starving." He stepped into the bedroom. "You wore me out. Now, you need to feed me."

His dark eyes roamed over her slinky, black dress.

"We ate a few hours ago." They'd had lunch delivered after her massage and they'd eaten naked in bed.

"A man can't live on pussy alone, although if I had to choose—"

"I wasn't talking about that." She wound her hair into a bun, her cheeks glowing red in the mirror. She wasn't entirely sure the blush was from his crass words. The throbbing between her legs was not an indicator of shyness.

"I can't remember eating anything else." He stepped into the bathroom, absorbing all the air with his large frame. It was the only excuse for her shallow breathing. "At least nothing as delicious." He stopped behind her, watching her in the mirror as his large hand ran under her dress and up to her ass. "You look amazing."

"We're not going to make it to dinner if you keep this up." And she didn't care one bit. Dinner, naked in bed, like lunch was fine with her.

"You're right." The heat in his eyes disappeared as he stepped away from her. "Let's go."

She blinked, staring at him in the mirror. That'd been unexpected. Once Terry's motor started humming, he was all systems go for foreplay and sex. Everything else could come later. No pun intended.

"You're done. You look great." He took her hand and tugged as he headed for the door.

"Ah…my hair." She stumbled after him.

"Lovely." He didn't even turn to look at her.

"Wait." She yanked on his hand.

He sighed as he let her go. "I'm going to perish from starvation."

"Oh, please. You aren't starving." She hurried back into the bathroom and added a tie around the bun to keep it in place. "There. All ready."

"Great." Terry dropped his arm to his side. He'd been looking at his watch all evening. "Let's go." He opened the door and let her proceed him into the hallway.

CHAPTER 13: TERRY

Terry escorted Maggie into the dining room and held her chair for her. Tonight was going to be perfect. He'd planned every detail—a great dinner, adult conversation with no kids and then mind-blowing sex.

The waiter was there immediately with water and their menus. As soon as Maggie wasn't looking, Terry grabbed his phone and texted the staff that they were out of the room. When dinner was over the Mobile Saint would be set up and waiting. His dick rose at the thought of her tied to the Saint, helpless, naked and at his mercy.

"What's good?" she asked from behind her menu.

"Everything." He didn't even glance at his.

"What do you recommend?" She lowered her menu, eyes on him.

"Everything is good. Really, it is."

"Everything? You've tried it all."

"Yeah." He shrugged. "Before I met you, I almost lived here."

"Oh, Terry." Her face softened.

He took her hand. "I…" In the middle of a dining room was not the place to confess his love. "I'm glad that I found you."

"Me too." She squeezed his hand. "I love you."

His throat tightened so much he almost choked but he covered it with a cough. "Ah…I'm having the Mahi. I don't want anything too heavy." He lifted her hand and kissed it, ignoring the shadow of hurt in her gaze. "I don't want to be sleepy. Not tonight."

She smiled but it didn't reach her eyes. She pulled her hand from his and looked back at her menu. "I think I'll have the soup and salad then."

The waiter came by. "May I interest you in some wine?"

"Glenlivet on the rocks. Maggie, would you like wine?"

"No." She picked up her glass. "Just water for me."

"I'll be right back with your scotch and some bread," said the waiter.

"I think we're ready to order." He had no intention of dallying in the Club tonight. It wouldn't take them long to get the Saint set up and he was more than eager to play.

"Excellent." The waiter took their order and left.

"Does your head still hurt?" A headache could put a damper on his evening but he'd read that sex actually helped to get rid of a headache.

"A little." She touched her temple.

"I'm sorry. I forget that you aren't as used to drinking

38

as I am. Next time, I'll make sure you don't overdo it."

"Is next time tonight?".

"No. Tonight is just us."

The tension fled her shoulders. "Good. I mean last night was lovely but—"

"That it was." Richard stopped at the table. "Maggie. Terry. How nice to see you."

CHAPTER 14: MAGGIE

Maggie wanted to crawl under the table and hide. Richard had seen her naked. No, not just naked, he'd seen her orgasm and touch herself and...Oh God, she couldn't look at him.

"Richard." Terry stood, shaking the other man's hand. "Why don't you join us?"

Maggie's mouth dropped open and her eyes shot to Terry's. The ass gave her a sexy smirk, his brow rising in challenge.

"I'd love to but I can't."

Praise the lord.

"I'm meeting a friend for dinner."

"Is he here?" Terry looked around.

"No, she hasn't arrived yet." Richard glanced at his watch. "I'm a little early."

"Then please, join us until she arrives." Terry waved over the waiter. "I'll buy you a drink."

Maggie was going to kill him and not a judge on the

planet, at least not a female judge, would find her guilty. It'd be justifiable homicide. No doubt about that.

"Thank you." Richard sat and ordered a drink before turning toward her. "Maggie, you look lovely tonight."

"Thank you." *As lovely as last night when you saw me naked, or lovelier because my clothes hide my fat butt.* She didn't say it but no matter how hard she tried she couldn't stop that mean voice inside her head. She heard it less often now but it was always there, waiting for a weak moment.

"What new pleasures do you have planned for your little Sub tonight?" Richard turned toward Terry.

Terry's dark eyes heated. "The Mobile Saint."

"Oh. That's always fun." Richard nodded, his eyes turning more blue than grey as he glanced at her.

"What's that?" She was pretty sure that nothing in this Club should have the word saint associated with it.

"She's never?" Richard looked at Terry.

"Nope. Never even seen one, I'd bet."

"Are you inviting guests?" Richard looked hopeful.

Maggie swallowed, waiting on Terry's response. He'd said it'd be only the two of them tonight but he did like an audience.

"No." He took her hand and kissed it. "Tonight is just for us."

"I won't say I'm not disappointed but I understand." Richard turned toward her. "*You* are in for quite a treat tonight, Maggie May."

"What is this...Mobile Saint?"

"You'll find out when we return to our room."

"It's in our room?" Her mind scrambled for anything saintly in their suite but everything had been normal—bed, table, chairs—nothing wicked or saintly that she'd seen.

"It's not there yet but it will be soon."

"I...I don't understand."

"They're setting it up while we have dinner." His phone beep and he glanced at it. "Actually, it's ready now."

"Is that why you were in such a hurry to leave?"

"It is." His thumb caressed the top of her hand, sending sparks sizzling through her body. "Otherwise, I would've been happy to stay in our room all night." He kissed her knuckles. "Maybe next time but tonight we're going to relive an evening from our past in La Petite Mort Club style."

"Which night?" Her mind tumbled through all the kinky, glorious things she'd done with him.

"One from early in our relationship but I'll tell you more later. Right now, we're being rude to our guest." He grinned and dropped her hand. "So Richard, how's that acquisition of the edible six pack holder going?"

It was sweet that he wanted to recreate a night from their past but which one? The big jerk was doing this on purpose, teasing her and making her wonder and wait. It was almost as bad as when he delayed her orgasm.

"That? I bought that company months ago. You've been out of touch." Richard's eyes darted to Maggie. "Lucky man that you are."

"I am that." Terry's gaze skimmed over her, making

her heart melt.

He cared for her. She could see it in his eyes, but was fondness for her all that he felt? Her stomach twisted. He was going to destroy her heart one day and there was nothing she could do about it.

"Excuse me." Richard stood. "My friend is here."

Maggie turned as the most beautiful woman—young woman—she'd ever seen walked over to them. She had black hair, a perfect body and an exotically, beautiful face.

"Maggie, Terry, this is Desiree," said Richard.

"Nice to meet you." Maggie held out her hand, hoping the smile on her face didn't look fake as her gaze landed on the bracelet. Desiree worked here as a…What did Ethan call them? Pleasure Associate.

"Nice to meet you." Desiree shook her hand turning to Terry who'd stood when she'd walked up to the table. "And you too."

"Yes, nice to meet you." He shook Desiree's hand quickly before dropping it.

His words and tone had been normal but the tension around his mouth and the hint of panic in his eyes made Maggie's gut clench. It was the same half-pissed off and half-terrified look her ex had gotten when they'd bumped into Stephanie at the store. At the time, Maggie hadn't known the two were having an affair but she'd never forgotten the look on David's face. It was like he was angry with both her and Stephanie but also scared shitless.

Terry wore the identical expression and that meant he knew Desiree intimately, but why hide it? As a long-standing member of the Club, he'd probably slept with many of the women here. He'd never acted embarrassed about his past before…unless Desiree wasn't his past. No. He was home every night. *Sex can happen during the day too*. That voice again. She hated it but it had a point. She had to know.

"Why don't the two of you join us for dinner." She smiled up at them, hoping the fear wasn't visible on her face. "I'd love to get to know another woman here. So far, I've only met men."

Richard turned to Desiree. "Would you like—"

"I'm sure they'd like to be alone," said Terry.

Richard looked from one to the other and Desiree seemed just as unsure on how to proceed.

"Please. I insist." She motioned to the chairs. "It'll be nice having adult company for once."

"They have other plans." Terry frowned at her but his eyes darted to the side, tearing her heart in two.

"Oh. Yes. Of course." Her stomach twisted. He'd cheated on her with…with this young, thin, beautiful woman. This was her ex all over again. She had to get out of there before she cried. She smiled but her lips trembled. "Excuse me. I need to use the rest room." She hurried away before she broke into tears.

CHAPTER 15: TERRY

"Damn it." Terry stared after Maggie's retreating form. He had nothing to hide. He hadn't done anything with Desiree but he still felt guilty.

"I apologize. I didn't know the two of you were familiar with one another," said Richard.

"We aren't. Not in the way you think." He had to fix this but the truth wasn't going to paint him in a good light.

The waiter came by with their dinner.

"I think this is our cue to leave," said Richard.

"It's probably best if you do." He stared in the direction of the bathroom, his mind spinning on how to convince Maggie that nothing had happened between Desiree and him without divulging everything that had and without lying. He wouldn't lie to her. Ever.

"Terry," said Desiree. "If I can do anything to help, let me know." She smiled softly. "She may be more willing to believe me. I have no reason to lie."

"Thanks, but I'll handle it."

"Of course." She touched his arm. "I'm glad the two of

you made up. You certainly look happier than that other night."

"I am." He glanced back at the restroom door. Maggie headed toward their table; a placid expression plastered on her face like a mask. "Or I was." He had a funny feeling he'd have to work hard to earn his happiness tonight.

"Good luck," said Richard as he and Desiree walked across the restaurant to an empty table.

Maggie sat. "Oh, this looks good." She smiled at him but it was brittle.

"It's not what you think."

"It isn't?" She looked at him, eyes wide but still bright from tears. "It sure looks like soup and salad."

"That's not...Is that how you want to play this?"

"I'm not playing anything." She took a bite of soup. "Oh, this is good."

"Fine." He cut a piece of fish and ate it. It was delicious. Probably. Should be. Everything here was, but right now he couldn't tell because all he could taste was trouble.

CHAPTER 16: MAGGIE

Maggie tried to focus on her food but her stomach twisted into a knot of hurt, anger and uncertainty. She couldn't go through this again. She wouldn't. She didn't want to know the truth but she wasn't going to sit here and pretend nothing was wrong. "Are you still sleeping with her." Her words were whisper soft—scared that this weekend which was supposed to be the start of a new aspect to their life was actually going to be its end.

"Excuse me?" Terry's fork froze on its way to his mouth.

"You heard me." She looked up at him.

"I thought you didn't want to talk about it."

"I changed my mind." She put down her spoon and wiped her mouth on the napkin.

"Okay." He put his fork on his plate in a measured movement. She'd seen him do this hundreds of times. He was stalling, gathering his words, twisting and forming them in his mind so they came out exactly like he wanted. So, they painted the picture he wanted her to see. "I have never slept with her."

"Desiree?" She wasn't going to let him guide her to his conclusion. She was going to make him answer her questions and that meant being very specific.

"Yes."

"You didn't sleep with her?" Hope flared in her chest. Terry may manipulate words but he never lied.

"Never." His gaze shifted away from hers.

It was a quick trip, a slight movement but it was enough to shatter her hope. He may not be lying but he wasn't being completely honest either. Language was his tool, his job. He made it dance to his tune and she was done with that.

"I'm sorry. Let me be more specific." She leaned closer. "Are you still fucking her."

His eyes widened.

"And I don't mean at this exact moment but at other times, when we're not together are you having sex with that woman?"

"No." He stared at her for a long moment before glancing down. He tried to cover it by moving his fork but she knew.

She took a deep breath. "Terry, if you did something with her before we met, that's fine. I know you spent a lot of time here. I know you've slept...had sex with many of the members and the women who work here. Just tell me."

"You want me to tell you about each woman I've fucked?" He shook his head. "No. I'm not doing that. It won't be good for you or for me. The past is the past."

"You're right. I don't need to know about every woman you've been with." Her gut twisted. He'd been a member here for years. The number of beautiful, thin, successful women he'd slept with must be in the hundreds.

"Good." He took another bite of his fish, eyeing her warily.

She ate some more, the food like cardboard in her mouth. She should let it go but she couldn't. "But I do want to know about Desiree."

"Damn it, Maggie. Let it go." He dropped his fork, tossed back his scotch and waved over the waiter. "I need another drink."

"And a rum and coke for me."

"I thought you weren't drinking tonight."

"You were wrong." She smiled, trying to force the tears back. "But so was I. About a lot of things." She put her napkin on the table and stood. "Excuse me." She turned and walked away. She was not going through this again. He was hiding something. If he hadn't slept with Desiree, he'd wanted to. He probably had his affair planned to the smallest detail. *Why would he bother with an affair? They weren't married. He'd just leave and why shouldn't he? Desiree was young and beautiful. Unlike her.* God, she hated that voice almost as much as she hated Terry right now.

CHAPTER 17: TERRY

Damn, damn, and double damn. Terry hated when Maggie cried but he couldn't tell her about what had happened between him and Desiree. And for fuck's sake, she should trust him. He was home with her every damn night. Where would he find the time or stamina to fuck someone else?

Maggie kept going straight. That wasn't the way to the bathroom. She walked out of the restaurant and into the Club. Damn it. He stood as the waiter stopped at his table. "Put this on my tab." He tossed downed his drink and went after her.

By the time he got to the door, she was gone. He scanned the crowd. There she was—back straight and pace fast. He maneuvered through the people. She turned, heading for the back rooms.

He started to holler but that'd draw everyone's attention and he didn't need that. People were already looking. Seeing Subs run from their Doms wasn't usual, but this was about more than his reputation. "Maggie, wait!"

Everyone turned and looked at him, except her. She just stiffened slightly and kept walking.

"Oh, no," he mumbled. "You aren't getting away that easily." He lengthened his stride and caught up with her at the door to their suite.

"Maggie, wa..." He clamped his mouth shut. He wanted to go into their room. He could talk to her there—touch her, make her see that he didn't want anyone but her. Plus, the Mobile Saint was waiting for them. His cock rose, eager to see her strapped down and at his mercy.

She opened the door and walked inside, heading for the bedroom. He followed and almost ran into her as she stopped in the doorway.

"Oh my God, what were you planning on doing? Crucifying me?"

He laughed. "Kind of but not in a bad way."

"There's a good way to crucify someone?" She glared at him over her shoulder.

"Yes." His hands landed on her shoulders, pulling her flush against him, her ass cradling his cock. "One filled with pleasure."

"Well, that's not going to happen tonight." She jerked away from him and walked to the closet. "Or ever."

"Maggie, I swear I never had sex with Desiree."

"Then what are you hiding?"

"We never did anything." He crossed his hand over his heart. "I promise."

"That's not what I asked." She pulled her suitcase from the closet and dropped it on the bed.

"What are you doing?" His words were a whisper and a warning of his pending temper.

"What does it look like?"

"Put it away." This was not going to happen. She wasn't going ruin their weekend because of a non-issue.

"No." She walked to the dresser and pulled out a stack of her clothes.

"I'm not fucking kidding. Put the suitcase away."

She ignored him, stuffing her clothes inside the case.

"I said stop." He strode across the room and grabbed the suitcase.

"Terry, give that to me."

He didn't bother to reply as he walked to the dresser and lifted it over the drawer.

"Don't you dare."

He raised his brow and tipped the case, her clothes falling in a jumble into the drawer and onto the floor.

"You're an ass." She almost spat the words.

"And you're being irrational." He dropped the suitcase.

"Irrational?" Her voice raised a level.

"Yes." He took two steps and pulled her into his arms. "I never slept with her."

"Slept?" She was stiff in his arms.

He sighed. "I never fucked her. Is that what you want to hear?" He ran his hands up and down her back, trying to sooth away her anger. "I haven't had sex with anyone since you."

"Really?" Her gaze held his and some of the tension slipped from her body.

"Yes." He bent to kiss her but stopped as her eyes narrowed. Only an idiot or a blind man would attempt to kiss a woman who was looking at him like that.

"Then what *did* you do with her?"

"Nothing. I swear." He stepped away. She was getting too close to the truth. "You need to stop acting like this."

"Stop acting...Oh, no." She poked his chest. "You don't get to do this. You've pushed me and changed me. I'm not the same person I was and I'm not going to sit back and do nothing while you have an affair. I did that with David but I'm not doing it with you."

"An affair? When would I find time for an affair?" He threw up his hands. "I'm with you every night. We fuck all the time."

"Not as much as you want. The kids are always around. Is that why you come here? Is that what you tell yourself? That it's okay because you wouldn't have an affair if I could have sex with you whenever you wanted."

"How many times do I have to tell you? I'm not cheating on you," he said through clenched teeth.

She laughed. It was a brittle, humorless sound. "Why because it's just sex? Just a blow job?" She wiped her eyes. "Let me tell you that it's never just sex for us. Not for women. When you men cheat—"

"God damn it, Maggie. I'm not having sex with anyone but you."

"It hurts." She jabbed him in the chest again. "It always hurts and I'm done being hurt by men." She turned, heading for the door.

"I didn't do anything." He grabbed her arm. "Fucking listen to me."

"Red, Terry. Red."

His hand dropped to his side. "Maggie, don't do this."

"Red." She hiccupped, tears running down her cheeks. "Goodbye, Terry." She opened the door.

"You want to know what happened?" His voice was so soft he barely heard it but she stopped. "Fine. I'll tell you." Fuck, he didn't want to do this but he couldn't lose her. "When we broke up, I went to a room with Desiree but we didn't do anything." He walked past her into the living room and over to the bar. He was going to need a drink for this conversation because his rabbit wasn't going to stop until she'd pulled every humiliating detail from him.

"Nothing?"

"What difference does it make? We were broken up. You hadn't called to apologize. I didn't think I'd ever see you again." He took a large gulp of his scotch, watching her and preparing to duck if she threw something at him.

CHAPTER 18: MAGGIE

"So, this is my fault?" She followed Terry into the living room. The man was unbelievable.

"Yes," Terry almost growled. "You were being stupid about the house."

"Don't call—"

"I'm not calling you stupid. I said you were acting stupid."

"Same thing."

"It is not. How many times…" He snapped his jaw shut, the muscle in his cheek throbbing. "We were broken up. What I did shouldn't matter."

"So, you did have sex with her?" She crossed her arms over her chest.

"No and that's why this fight is so fucking stupid." He started to pace. "We should be having sex right now and instead you're pissed at me for something I almost did when we were broken up."

"Almost?"

"Shit."

"Yeah, shit." She knew it. He'd cheated on her. Maybe he hadn't done the deed but in his head and heart, he'd cheated.

"We were broken up," he shouted.

That didn't matter. He'd wanted to have sex with another woman—a young, beautiful, thin woman and..."You lied to me."

"I never fucking lied to you."

"The first time we were together after that fight you said you hadn't been with anyone else." She'd been scared that he had but she'd been willing to forgive him.

"And I hadn't." He stared at the ceiling as if hoping for divine intervention but when none came, he looked back at her. "Why can't you understand that? I have never fucked anyone but you since the night we met."

Her heart softened but she couldn't let this go. He was keeping something from her and she wasn't going to be a fool like she'd been with her ex. "Then why were you acting so strange around her?" She moved closer to him. "Something happened and you feel guilty about it. Did she give you a blow job?" The thought of Desiree touching him made her want to slap Terry, tear out the young woman's eyes and curl into a ball and cry.

"No." He looked away.

"You went down on her." They'd been broken up. She'd had no claim to him. It shouldn't hurt so much but it did.

"I didn't touch her, kiss her or eat her pussy. I swear."

56

His eyes kept darting over her shoulder.

"If you'd told me when we'd first gotten back together, I would've been okay with it, but you didn't." She stared up at him, her heart shattering at the pain on his handsome face. "You want me to trust you. To obey you. You want to be my Dom but how can I trust you when you're hiding things from me?" She swallowed, trying not to fall apart. Not yet. Not in front of him. "I...I can't be with someone I don't trust."

"You're fucking kidding me?" His eyes searched her face. "Maggie..."

"Don't." She shook her head. "I'm not that woman anymore. I won't sit by why you cheat on me."

"I am not cheating on you." He grabbed her shoulders. "I have *never* cheated on you. I *will* never cheat on you."

"How can I believe you when you won't tell me the truth?" She waited, hoping and praying he'd tell her and it'd be something she could believe; something she could forgive.

"Fuck." He dropped his hands. "You want the truth?"

"Yes." She did and didn't. She wouldn't stay with a man who'd cheated on her, no matter how sorry he was. She'd done that before but never again.

"I went with her to the back." He turned away, his voice soft, defeated. "I had every intention of fucking her because I wanted to forget, for a few moments, about you."

"Do not blame this on me."

He spun around, his dark eyes blazing with anger. "I'm blaming you because it's your fault. Your fault that I was alone with one of the most beautiful women I've ever seen and…"

"And what?" The words came out scratchy from holding back the tears. He'd been alone with her. With the most beautiful, young woman he'd ever seen. She didn't want to know what he'd say next, but she had to.

"She gave me a back massage and I passed out."

"A back massage? What does that mean?" It had to be something kinky.

"It means she rubbed my back."

"Like today? Like you gave me a back massage?"

"No. Nothing like today." He ran his hand through his hair. "It was just a massage. Nothing else."

"I don't believe you." It wasn't even a good lie. No man, especially one like Terry, would be alone with a woman as beautiful as Desiree for a back massage when he could pay her for anything.

"Well, it's the truth"

She studied him but he walked to the bar and refilled his drink. She turned and grabbed her purse, pulling out her phone.

"Who are you calling?" He strode over to her.

"An Uber. I'm going home. We can talk when you're ready to tell me the truth."

"I am telling you the truth." He snatched the phone from her.

"Give me that."

"No." He held it in the air out of her reach.

"Go to hell, Terry." She headed for the door.

"Where are you going?" He followed her.

"Someone will give me a ride."

"Wait." He grabbed her arm.

"Red." She glared at his hand as she opened the door.

"Damn it. Stop saying your Safeword." He dropped his hold. "Don't do this, Maggie."

"I'm not. You are." Only her rage kept her from falling to the ground and sobbing. She'd known he'd hurt her one day but she hadn't expected this tearing pain where her heart had been.

"I couldn't get it up."

"What?" She couldn't have heard that correctly.

He dropped his hand and walked to the bar, grabbing the bottle of scotch and taking a swig.

"What did you say?"

"You heard me." He dropped onto the couch, bottle in hand. "Don't make me repeat it."

"You…you couldn't?" She closed the door and walked toward him. Terry had never, ever had that issue with her.

"No."

"It happens." She sat next to him and touched his arm.

"Not to me."

But it had and she couldn't be happier, except… "And that's why you didn't fuck her."

"Yeah."

She stood. "Would you have told me if you had…been able to?"

"Yes, I would've." He looked up at her. "We were

broken up. I have nothing to apologize for."

"You can start with keeping this from me."

"Nothing happened."

"You almost had sex with another woman and you didn't tell me. You should've told me."

"It wasn't something I wanted to talk about, especially with you."

"Me? Why? Because you knew I'd be hurt? Because you knew not telling me was lying? Because you knew you were wrong? Not having sex because you were too drunk is the same as cheating?"

"How in the name of fuck is being a limped-dicked eunuch the same as cheating? It's the opposite of cheating."

"Not when the intention was there. The only reason you didn't have sex with her was because you drank too much."

He rested his forehead against the bottle and laughed, a hollow sound without a hint of joy. "Oh, I wish that were the reason. That would've been so simple. I could've slept, sobered up and then fucked her."

Something about the defeat in his slumped shoulders and voice made her heart soften. They had been broken up. She sat on the couch, close but not close enough to touch. She wasn't ready for that yet. "Why didn't you do that?"

He moved the bottle, his eyes locking with hers. "Because sleep wouldn't have changed anything."

"I don't understand. You would've been sober."

"And sober, all I could think of was you. I drank to

forget you. To forget that I'd just lost the best thing that'd ever happened to me."

"Terry…" Lord, help her. She couldn't stay mad at him when he said things like that. She reached for him, wanting to take away his sorrow.

"I love you, Maggie." His dark eyes were haunted, scared and yet filled with so much hope.

"What?" She had to be dreaming but this wasn't exactly the romantic confession of love she'd imagined.

"This wasn't how I wanted to tell you." He glanced away.

"What did you say, Terry." She had to hear it again to believe it. She wanted it so badly she may have imagined it. She clutched her hands together to stop herself from grabbing him and either shaking him or kissing him. Right now, she wasn't sure which she'd do.

CHAPTER 19: TERRY

"I love you, Maggie." Terry swallowed, the bottle shaking in his hands. "I didn't want to. I never wanted to love anyone again but I do." Fuck, he'd made a cluster of this whole thing.

"You love me? Really?"

His heart raced, fear causing a cold sweat to break out across his skin but the uncertainty and hope in her eyes gave him the courage to continue. "Yes. I have for a long ti..."

Maggie launched herself at him, her arms wrapping around his neck and her lips covering his. He tightened his hold on her and kissed her, his tongue tangling with hers as his love turned into hot need. He had to claim this woman and show her what he couldn't say—show her how much he needed her, loved her. He cupped her face, holding her for his kiss. "Maggie." It was a plea.

She tugged at his shirt, pulling it from his pants, her hands skimming up his chest and making his nuts tighten.

He shoved her dress and bra out of his way before his mouth attached to her breast—the nipple already hard for him. She moaned, arching into him, her hands tangling in his hair. He rubbed between her thighs as he sucked her breast. He needed her as desperate for him as he was for her.

"Oh, Terry. Please." She rocked against his hand, her underwear already damp.

He had to be inside her, claim her as his. He shifted, pushing her to her back and pulling her underwear to the side. He didn't have time to take them off. He needed her now. He unzipped his pants, pulling out his cock and sliding the tip against her slick heat. He rubbed it along her clit, making her moan and writhe beneath him. Her legs wrapped around him, her heels pushing on his ass, hurrying him along. He slid inside her, taking his time, savoring the way she clung to him, pulling him deeper until he was sheathed all the way.

"I love you." He stilled, his eyes locking with hers as he pushed her hair from her face.

She touched his cheek, her gaze overflowing with wonder and love. "I love you too."

He kissed her, softly. Now, that he was inside her, his hurry had vanished. She was his. No one could doubt that with his dick buried so deep in her they were one. "I love you." He said again, kissing her cheeks and lips. "I'm going to tell you that every day for the rest of our lives."

"Good." She ran her hands through his hair and tugged him to her lips, her tongue darting into his mouth and exploring, making his blood hum. "But can you show me?" She smiled as she tightened her inner muscles, squeezing his cock and making the air leave him in a hiss.

"Absolutely." Words were done for now. He pulled out of her. Her soft whimper of protest, making him feel like a king. She loved his cock and she loved him. He lifted on one arm, watching as his dick disappeared inside her over and over. He made love to her, slow and steady, letting her know that they'd be together forever.

"Terry, please." Her fingers clutched at his arm as her legs tightened around him, trying to keep him buried deep inside her.

"Patience, rabbit." He whispered, kissing her again as he pushed into her, a little faster, a little harder. His balls protested the pace, wanting to race to completion, but he gritted his teeth as he slowly danced her closer and closer to the edge.

CHAPTER 20: MAGGIE

Maggie shifted under Terry, her heart overflowing at his gentleness and care. She loved this man but she needed to come.

He brushed the hair from her face, his dark eyes filled with love as he slowly slid inside her. She melted at the warmth in his gaze. She'd cherish this moment and that look forever. His body shifted, retreating from her again, leaving her wanting and empty.

"Terry, please." Her fingers dug into his arms.

"Please what?" A slow smile spread across his handsome face, knowing exactly what she wanted.

"You know." She pulled him closer with her feet.

"I thought you enjoyed slow love making." He grinned as he continued his relentless pace, in and almost all the way out before filling her again.

"I do." It was lovely and wonderful, making her body warm but that spark of flame wouldn't light. She needed friction for the fire that'd make her explode. "But I need more."

"Patience, rabbit." He bent licking her nipple and sending electricity straight to her pussy.

One hand clung to his arm while the other tangled in his hair, holding his head to her chest. His kissed all around her breast, coming close but not touching her nipple.

"Please." She yanked on his hair, trying to steer him closer.

"My little rabbit isn't obeying." He smiled against her breast and before she could protest his mouth was on her nipple, sucking at the same time he thrust into her, hard and fast.

She gasped, her back arching, offering her breasts as her pussy clamped down on him. The sparks, once only flickers, ignited as he teased her nipple with tongue and teeth, sending pleasure shooting to her core. He grabbed her ass, pulling her upward so they were face to face on the couch. He lifted her leg, opening her more fully to his thrusts as his hands squeezed her thighs.

"I love you." This time he thrust into her hard.

She gasped as that flame turned into an inferno but he wasn't even close to done. He pumped into her harder and faster, pushing her against the arm of the couch with his force. She wrapped her arms around his back, clinging to him. He was the only safety in the storm of passion and fire that consumed her. She cried out as his lips found her neck, sucking hard before soothing with his tongue. She needed more. Her nails dug into his shoulders as she tried to pull him closer, trying to make them one. His breath in her ear came in pants, his thrusts desperate. He straightened her leg even more as his dick rocked inside her, faster and harder, barely even leaving her body. She shattered, clenching onto him and making him grunt, his body out of control as he held her still. He pushed into her hard and fast before exploding inside her, filling her with his love. He stiffened, groaning in her ear and burying his face in her neck.

She ran her hand across his shoulder. "I love you," she whispered, no longer hesitant about saying the words because only happiness came with them now.

CHAPTER 21: TERRY

Terry drifted in and out of a satiated daze, his hand skimming up and down Maggie's back. He should strip off her clothes so he could touch her skin but he didn't want to do anything to interrupt this peacefulness. At some point, he'd rolled over and had pulled her on top of him but they'd both been too close to their orgasm to want to talk. He wasn't sure that'd still be the case now. He was a lawyer, arguing came naturally to him but he hated talking about his feelings and he was pretty sure he was in for a grilling.

She shifted, leaning up on his chest, her hazel eyes bright with love and it made his stomach twist and his heart swell. Fuck, he didn't want to screw this up.

"So, how long have you—"

"Wanted you?" His hand drifted down to her ass. "Since the moment I saw you. That ill-fitting red dress highlighted your tits exceptionally well. I swear, I held my breath several times, hoping they'd pop out."

"Stop it." She slapped his chest. "That's not what I was going to ask and you know it."

He sighed. "I don't know, Maggie." He shifted, rolling out from under her. "I love you. Can't that be enough?" He tucked his dick back into his pants and zipped up. Apparently, it was time for her two thousand and more questions.

"Yeah. I guess." Her eyes dimmed.

"Damn it." He was messing up already. He captured her chin. "I'm not good at talking about this stuff. You know that." He kissed her softly.

"I know." She swallowed. "It's fine."

Now, he felt like an ass. "It's not fine. If you really want to hear how I feel and all that crap, I'll try and tell you." He ran his thumb over her cheek. "It won't be what you're hoping to hear. I'm not prone to eloquence or romance, but I'll do my best to answer you honestly."

"Thank you." Her eyes shone brighter and his heart swelled so much his chest hurt.

"God, I love you." He kissed her again and her arms wrapped around his neck, holding him close as she melted against him. He broke away, his chest heaving. "Oh, no. Not yet. We still have some games to play."

"We do?" Her eyes widened, sparkling with curiosity.

"Oh yeah. We do. You may have spoiled how I was going to declare my love for you but you are not thwarting my plans for tonight." He took her hand and tugged. It seemed her inquisitive nature had saved him from her two thousand questions, at least for now. "I spent way too much time putting everything together for this to not happen."

"You did?" She stood, straightening her dress.

"Yep." He led her toward the bedroom.

"You've fantasized about crucifying me? I'm not sure I'm comfortable with that." She smiled at him.

"Good. Comfortable is not a word to describe anything about the Mobile Saint." He stopped and moved behind her. "Exhilarating. Pleasurable. Torturous. Orgasmic. But never comfortable."

"Torturous?"

"Only in a good way." He unzipped her dress and removed the tie from her hair. Her ran his fingers through her soft curls, watching as they cascaded down around her shoulders. He tugged and she moaned softly, making his dick harden even more. If he didn't stop touching her, they'd be fucking again and it wasn't time for that, not yet. "Go stand in front of the Saint."

"Bra?"

"Hmm." He pursed his lips. "Let's go with off. Underwear too."

She reached behind her back and he waited. He'd never tire of seeing her tits escape her bra. The way they jiggled and swayed, knowing how soft and warm they were and how her nipples puckered under his tongue. He ran his hand over his dick as she dropped her bra. Her tits swayed as she pushed her panties down and kicked them aside.

"You're gorgeous."

She smiled shyly at him but didn't try to cover herself

or argue. She was learning.

"See those straps at the bottom of the posts?"

She looked down and nodded.

"Hook them around your ankles."

"You want me to do it?" Her large, hazel eyes widened with surprise.

"Yep." He leaned against the bed post. "I'm going to watch while you buckle yourself into the Saint Andrew's Cross."

CHAPTER 22: MAGGIE

Maggie bent, her butt brushing against the wood of the cross as she hooked the Velcro around first one ankle and then the other.

"Make sure they're tight. I don't want them coming loose at your first struggle," said Terry.

"Yes, Sir." She fought a smile as she tugged on the restraint, making sure her efforts made her breasts swing.

"That's it. Now the other one." His voice had grown gruff with his desire.

He liked seeing her breasts sway and his enjoyment meant her enjoyment. She doubled her efforts, pulling on the other strap several times so her breasts jiggled. Then she straightened slowly, running her hands up her legs as she did. She stopped, fingers resting on her inner thighs. "It's very tight, Sir."

"I bet it is." Terry pulled off his shirt, baring all that smooth, muscular flesh as he leaned against the wall. His eyes were black with desire and focused on the juncture between her legs.

"It is, Sir, but perhaps you want to see for yourself." She tried to keep her expression innocent but they both knew they weren't talking about the restraints anymore.

"Perhaps I should."

"Whatever you want, Sir."

"Tempting the devil tonight, rabbit." His nostrils flared as his gaze traveled slowly up her body, leaving an inferno of lust in their wake.

"Just trying to please my Sir."

"You always please me." His eyes softened as he strode forward.

Her body melted, waiting on his touch, but instead of testing her *tightness*, he captured her wrist. He lifted her arm above her head and to the side, strapping it into the Velcro strap. He grabbed her other wrist, the hair on his chest rubbing against her breasts and making her nipples pucker even more.

"There. That's better." He stepped back, eyes roaming over her. "How do the restraints feel?"

She tugged on her arms. "Good."

"Not too tight?"

"No."

He captured her chin. "Let me know if they rub or scrape."

"Yes, Sir."

He took another step back, his eyes roaming over her body and leaving sparks in their wake. She was his prisoner. Naked. Her legs spread and tied to the two lower beams of the Saint Andrew's Cross, which looked like a big X, her arms secured to the upper two beams.

"Now, I can do anything I want to you and you can't even squirm to get away."

He was right about that and the anticipation made her throb. She wanted this man more than air.

"What to do first?" He continued to stare, making her breath hitch in her chest.

Terry planned everything. Sometimes he veered from those plans in the heat of the moment like last night and their fight tonight, but there was no way he didn't have every detail of this night prepared.

"Do you have a suggestion?"

"Whatever would make you happiest, Sir." She smiled at him. Tonight, she'd do her best to play the perfect Sub.

"Excellent choice." He grinned. "In that case, I think we'll get right to the surprise."

"There's more?" She'd thought this was the surprise.

"Oh, yeah." He walked behind the Mobile Saint. "Time to get you ready for our walk, or should I say our fuck, down memory lane."

A motor hummed and the boards shook slightly as the wood behind her tipped backward.

"Terry, I'm falling." She tried to stand, to get free but she couldn't.

"Nonsense. You're reclining." He cupped her cheek. "Trust me, Maggie."

"I do." She relaxed as the Mobile Saint shifted. He

wouldn't let her fall, not here and not in life. The machine stopped when she was flat on her back.

"That's better." He kissed her, his tongue tangling with hers as his hand skimmed down her belly and between her legs. "Nice and wet. Ready for my cock."

"Yes, Sir." She was always ready for him.

"Good, but that treat's for after we recreate our first dessert together."

"Our first dessert?" She had no idea what he was talking about.

"Cherries, rabbit. How could you forget?"

"Oh. The frozen cherries from work." Her body went into overdrive, almost combusting as memories of what they'd done that night flashed through her mind.

"Yes." He strode toward the kitchen and came back a moment later carrying two bowls full of the largest cherries she'd ever seen.

CHAPTER 23: MAGGIE

Terry used his foot to push a small end table next to the Saint Andrew's Cross before setting the bowls down. He picked up a cherry. It was large and dark red with chocolate on the bottom. "Would you like one, rabbit?"

"Ah…" How was he going to give it to her? Last time, he'd done the most wonderful things with those cherries.

He popped it into his mouth and chewed. "Delicious." He grabbed another one. "Try one. They're very good."

"Okay." It did look yummy but she wanted more than fruit.

"Open up."

She did and his eyes darkened as he gazed at her. He put it between his lips and bent until he was only a breath away from her mouth. She waited but he didn't move and then his hand trailed up her inner thigh.

He pulled the cherry from his lips with his other hand. "Say please." He put it back between his teeth as his fingers brushed over her pussy, soft and fleeting.

"Please, Sir." She wasn't asking for the cherry.

He bit down, letting half of the fruit fall into her mouth. It was delicious but not near as good as the fingers that teased between her legs.

"How was it?"

"Very good." She licked her lips, making sure her tongue skimmed over his mouth.

"Tease. You'll pay for that." His eyes sparkled as he leaned away from her. "Hmm. You've got some juice here."

He bent, his mouth capturing the side of hers, his tongue tickling at the corner of her lips. She opened for him and he kissed her quickly before pulling away.

"Not yet, rabbit." He walked into the kitchen. "First, we're going to play a game and you'd better pay attention."

Her body hummed. She loved his games. "Yes, Sir. I will."

He grinned as he walked back to the Saint Andrew's Cross carrying a bottle of chocolate liqueur and a spray can of whipped cream.

Her nipples tightened and the throbbing need between her legs intensified as she imagined exactly where that whipped cream was going to go.

"I was only going to use the chocolate liqueur but since you don't want to drink today, I'll use the whipped cream too."

"The whipped cream is for me?" That wasn't what she'd thought he was going to do with it, but her eyes dropped to the large bulge in his pants. "I can't wait." Her own sweet cock-sicle.

"Too bad. As wonderful as having you lick whipped cream off my dick would be, that's not the game. Not now anyway."

"Oh." She had to admit, she was disappointed.

"Fuck, Maggie." He cupped her check. "I love you." He bent, his lips capturing hers. This kiss was hot and filled with desire, as his hand dipped between her legs, sliding one long finger inside her. "We haven't even started and you're so wet, so eager to suck my cock and fuck me." His mouth trailed downward toward her breast, blowing across her hard, little peak before he groaned and straightened. "But...that'll have to wait." His chest heaved as he turned and grabbed a cherry. He held it up. "Look at the bottom. Do you see anything unusual?"

"Yes. There's chocolate on it.".

"Yes, but it's also flat." He turned it. "And see how it's been hollowed out."

"Yes." She was getting a tad nervous. He'd gone to great pains to set this up and that meant he was going to take his time. Her pulse raced, dreading and anticipating the pleasure filled torture that was coming her way.

He grabbed the whipped cream and filled the cherry. "I'm going to place this on your body and I want you to hold still and not let it spill."

"What?" That wasn't possible.

"You heard me. Where should I put this one?" He tapped his chin with his finger. "How about here?" He placed it on the top of her breast.

"That's freezing." She jerked and the cherry rolled down her chest.

"Oh. Did I forget to mention that this bowl has been in the freezer?"

"I don't think you forgot," she muttered.

"Shame on me and now you've made a mess." He grinned down at her, his dark eyes heating her flesh. "Since, you're tied up, I guess I'm going to have to clean you up."

"Yes." Her breath came in pants as he lowered his face, running his tongue over the top of her breast and down, following the trail of whipped cream. He teased along her nipple, pulling it into his mouth as his hand slid between her legs. His thumb, slightly cold from the cherry, teased her clit, rubbing it soft and then faster and harder as he sucked on her nipple. He slid a finger inside her, curling it to stroke her G-spot with each thrust.

She moaned, arching toward him. She only needed a little more and she'd come. Another finger. More pressure on her clit. Anything. Then he straightened, pulling his hand from between her legs.

She gasped, her body tight and shaky. She bit her lip to keep from begging him to let her come because begging never worked when Terry was playing.

"What I also didn't have a chance to tell you is that every time you let a cherry fall, I'm going to bring you to the edge of orgasm and not let you come."

"You've got to be kidding me." She closed her eyes,

her body trembling. She was going to kill him.

CHAPTER 24: TERRY

Terry grinned down at his little rabbit. She was wound tight already. Tonight was going to be fun. "Let's start. Shall we?"

"No." Maggie glared up at him. "There's no way I can keep cherries on my body."

"Sure you can, rabbit. I had the bottoms made nice and flat just for you. And the fudge is both delicious and functional. As it warms up it'll stick to your skin." He smirked as he pulled one from the bowl. "Let's try a non-frozen one this time."

"Doubt it'll make much difference," she grumbled.

"I'll let you choose where I should put it." He filled it with whipped cream.

"Oh, you don't want to hear where I think you should put it."

He laughed. "Temper, rabbit." He bent, his lips capturing hers. She opened for him, letting him sooth and entice. Her generosity floored him. Even when miffed she was so fucking giving and open. "Now"—his breath whispered across her lip—"let me rephrase. Where would you like me to put this on *your* body?"

"I don't know, Terry."

He cleared his throat, reminding her of his title when they were playing.

"Sir, I don't think it'll make a difference."

"Your stomach it is then. Hold still." He lowered the cherry and placed it on her rounded belly, waiting a moment for her to get used to the slight chill from the refrigerator before moving his hand. "See. All balanced."

Her eyes were wide with surprise as she smiled at him.

"Now, another."

"Ter...Sir."

"Let's see how many you can balance."

"But...if they fall."

"Then I clean you up and you pay for each one."

"That's not fair."

He shrugged as he grabbed another cherry. "My game. My rules."

"You're a jerk."

He laughed, holding another whipped cream filled cherry. "That's probably the mildest thing you're going to call me tonight." He put this one a few inches above the other.

She held her breath, balancing the fruit before slowly letting out her air and breathing carefully. "I think if I can balance three, I win this round."

"No." He shook his head. "That's too easy. As soon as

I put the third one down, you'll say you won."

"Okay. How about I have to keep it on my body for one minute."

"Hmm." He studied her. "You know, I should say no. This is my game but I'm a fair guy." He tried not to smirk. Fuck fairness. He always played to win. "How about three cherries for three minutes?"

"Okay. I can do that."

Not with his help she couldn't. "I'll get my phone." He turned and headed for the living room, glancing over his shoulder. "Don't move."

"Jerk," she hollered and then gasped as one of the cherries swayed.

His breath caught, waiting for it to tumble, but it wiggled and then righted itself. "Lucky."

She grinned and he was sure his heart exploded with emotion. He'd never imagined that he'd love a woman like this. He was so completely and utterly fascinated by her that he should be terrified—he was terrified sometimes—but right now he was happier than he'd ever been.

"I'll be right back." He hurried into the living room and grabbed his phone before going back to the bedroom and stopping in the doorway. "Damn, I was hoping you would've lost them by now."

"Nope." Her breathing was steady and the cherries barely moved.

He walked back to her, placing his phone on the table by the bowls. She should know by now that it didn't matter how good she was he'd win this round and every round.

"Okay. This time chocolate liqueur."

"Sir, please." She bit her lip.

"I'm not budging. I want some chocolate on your body, not all whipped cream."

Her breath caught and his gaze darted to the cherries. They wobbled but she steadied her breathing and they stilled.

"Damn. You're better at this than I'd thought."

"Me too." She smiled shyly at him.

He filled the cherry with chocolate. Her confidence was growing every day, exposing her true self to him and making him love her more and more. His heart stuttered. He couldn't get bogged down with emotion. He had to focus on the game and her pleasure. "Where to put this one?"

She almost shivered as he lowered his hand toward her breast. "Is it frozen?"

"I'm not telling." He moved his hand lower.

"Please. Let me get ready."

"Nope." His eyes met hers. "You know, I'm very competitive."

"Please." She begged but the sparkle in her eyes told him she was enjoying this as much as he was. She'd enjoy it even more when he made her lose.

"Pussy. Yep, that's where this one is going." He put the frozen cherry on her mound.

"Ter...Sir, that's freezing." Her body twitched but the cherries stayed in place. "Set the timer."

He frowned. He'd been sure the cold in that spot would've made her lose at least one cherry. He grabbed his phone and set the timer.

"Let me see."

"You don't trust me?" He cocked a brow at her. "That's insulting."

"You're very competitive, remember?"

He showed her the phone. "Oh rabbit, you have no idea."

CHAPTER 25: MAGGIE

Maggie lay on the Saint Andrew's Cross trying to barely breath as the seconds ticked by. The yoga and Pilates classes she'd taken were helping her to focus and hold steady. The three cherries weren't even wiggling. She glanced at Terry. He was dealing with this better than expected. He didn't like it when his games went off script.

"My nose is very itchy." He scratched the side of his nose.

Her eyes narrowed. Here was the Terry she knew— hyper-competitive.

"Boy, time is sure going slowly." He faked a yawn.

"You are such an ass." A yawn built in her throat, threatening to make her inhale deeply. "I am not going to yawn. I don't need to yawn," she mumbled to herself.

"What's that?" He leaned toward her. "Speak up. Your lips are moving but I can't hear you."

"You don't need to hear me," she said through clenched teeth. This man was so annoying.

"Now Maggie, you know I always want to hear what you have to say." His dark eyes sparkled with humor.

"You have to be kidding? Half the time, you barely listen to me when I'm talking." The man was just like all the others when it came to that. She'd come home from work and tell him about her day and get nothing but grunts.

"That's your fault."

"How is that my..." She held her breath as the cherry on her pubic mound started to roll.

"Go on? What were you saying?" His dark gaze heated as he stared at the disobedient fruit.

The cherry settled. She couldn't let him make her lose focus. She clamped her mouth shut. She was done talking.

"I could make you answer, rabbit." His eyes met hers.

She shook her head slightly.

"You don't think I can?"

"How much time is left?" It'd seemed like at least an hour since he'd set the alarm.

Terry glanced at the phone. "A little under two minutes."

"No way. Let me see it."

"Your distrust wounds me deeply." He smirked as he held the phone where she could see it without moving. "You know, it beeps when the time is up."

She sent him a dirty look but refused to argue with the ass. She was going to beat him at his own game. Her lips curved in a half smile.

"Since you're talking again, what were you saying before?"

She wasn't answering that and she couldn't shrug so she lifted her brows as if to say, "Don't know."

"Can't remember?"

She shook her head slightly.

"Let me refresh your memory." He wandered to the bottom of the cross. "I said that it was your fault that I don't listen when you talk. You were about to politely ask me to explain even though you have absolutely no doubt that I'm right because I always am. Does that about sum it up?"

His handsome smirk set her blood on fire with both annoyance and because she knew him well enough to know he was down at the end of the cross for a reason. It was written all over his smug face.

"Well rabbit, it's your fault because whenever I'm around you I can't focus on anything but how much I want to touch you." His finger skimmed up the inside of her leg.

"Sir, stop." Her body, so used to the pleasure he gave it, began to quiver with need.

"And taste you." His breath teased along her leg as he bent.

She couldn't see him anymore. She'd have to lean up and that'd be the end of the cherries. His lips tickled her calf and she groaned softly, tensing in anticipation. She didn't have to see him. Her body knew what was coming and wetness pooled between her legs. He kissed her calf and moved upward, his tongue darting out to tease her flesh. He paused when he reached her thigh.

"That's cheat..." She moaned as he nipped her leg, sucking on her skin and slowly moving closer to her center.

His tongue tickled along her slit and she trembled, sending the cherries tumbling down her body and spilling cool liquid over her pussy.

The alarm rang.

"Ah, there's my chocolate." His voice was rich and dark, better than any chocolate she'd ever had.

CHAPTER 26: TERRY

Terry stared at the delicious treat waiting for him. The cherries had rolled onto the floor but the chocolate and cream had spilled down her body. She shivered beneath his mouth as he licked a trail across her skin where her thigh met her pussy. "Delicious," he murmured against her lower lips, already swollen with need for him.

"You cheated."

He glanced at her. She was leaning up the best she could, glaring at him.

"My game. My rules." He grabbed the heart-shaped O-ring on her collar. "Now, watch me eat my dessert."

Her hazel eyes widened, sparkling with desire and her breath caught making those luscious breasts quiver as he lowered his face to her pussy.

CHAPTER 27: MAGGIE

"But that's not fair." Maggie's body tensed as Terry lowered his head between her legs.

"Is that really a problem, rabbit?" His dark eyes locked with hers as his hot breath teased her pussy.

"Ah...yes." No. Right now, the problem was that he was still talking but she couldn't make things too easy for him. He already had her naked, tied to a cross and covered in whipped cream and chocolate liqueur.

"Really?" His sexy mouth turned up in a grin. "I think you're mad because you're sticky." His eyes dipped to her pussy. "I can help with that." He kissed her pubic mound, sucking and licking the chocolate liqueur from her skin.

Her head dropped back to her shoulders and her eyes closed in ecstasy as his tongue tickled her clit.

"I said watch me." He yanked on her collar.

She stared as his dark head lowered between her pale thighs. His shoulders were wide and bare, so much bigger than her. His strength and power didn't scare her, instead it made her wetter, softer for him.

"That's better." His gaze stayed on hers as his tongue teased its way to her slit. "Delicious." He lapped along her seam and the sides where her thighs met her pussy, searching out and devouring all the liqueur. He gave her thigh a soft kiss and then a nip. "I think I got it all."

"Oh…good." Damn it. She did not want him to stop.

"Now for your punishment."

"What?"

"You dropped three cherries." His thumb slid back and forth across her pussy, pressing on her clit for one glorious moment with each upward stroke.

"Be-because of you." Her breath came faster now, increasing with the rhythm of his thumb.

"Is that so?' He focused on her clit, swirling around it, over and over, faster and faster.

Her body trembled, surrendering to the approaching passion.

"I asked you a question, rabbit?" He pressed harder on her tiny nub.

"Yes." She had no idea what he'd asked but right now yes was the only answer she knew. Her hips undulated, rocking against his hand. She was almost there, just a little more.

"Punishment one done."

"No," she cried as he pulled his hand away.

He walked up to her and bent, kissing her hard, his tongue diving into her mouth. She yanked her arms, trying to wrap them around him, cling to him, rub on him, anything to find her release, but she couldn't move.

He kissed along her neck to her ear and whispered, "Two more to go."

"No. Please. Sir. Master. Please. I can't." She'd die. She'd burst into flames and incinerate if he brought her to the edge again and denied her a release.

"I'm sorry but you dropped three cherries. I told you the rules." He walked away and came back a moment later with his bag.

"The rules? You're making them up as you go." Her eyes widened and her pussy clenched as he brought out the flogger. She'd more than enjoyed the riding crop last night.

"No. You need to pay attention. I explained the rules. For every cherry you drop, I bring you close to orgasm and stop. That's it. Simple."

She couldn't focus on anything but the flogger and the sound it made—whoosh as it cut through the air with each flex of his arm. Would it hurt or would there be pleasure hidden under the pain like the crop? "But...but I would've made the three minutes if you hadn't—"

"You're the one who wanted the game timed and you never said I couldn't do whatever I needed to in order to win."

"But...that's cheating."

CHAPTER 28: TERRY

"Nope. My rules. My game." He grinned as he gently dragged the flogger across Maggie's abdomen, watching as her flesh quivered at the soft touch. So eager. So trusting and so fucking close to the edge of bliss that one fast slap with the toy on her pussy and it'd be done. "I'd love to make you come just with this." He slapped the flogger along her breasts and she moaned. "But not yet. Right now, you have to pay for dropping the cherries."

"Please." She pulled at the restraints as he glided the flogger between her legs.

"Please what, rabbit?"

"Please let me come, Sir. Please."

"No." He slapped her thigh hard enough to leave several pink slashes on her soft, warm flesh.

"Oh…" Her gasp turned into a moan as he slapped her again in the same spot.

"You must learn to obey, no matter how hard. No matter what I do."

"Yes, Sir." Her eyes were as green as the deep forest and her body as lush. She was a goddess of old—round, ripe and succulent.

He slapped the flogger across her abdomen, letting the tips of the lashes tap along her pussy.

"Oh...my...Terry." She almost sat upright.

"I think that was a little too close." He dropped the flogger and leaned down, kissing the pink along her thigh and abdomen, letting his tongue dart between her legs for a quick taste. She was dripping for him. She'd feel so slick and hot on his cock. His tongue slid inside her, his dick twitching and trying to escape his pants when her muscles spasmed under his mouth. She was close. He only had a few more seconds. His mouth moved to her clit as he slid two fingers inside her.

She moaned, low and loud, making his dick almost burst through his pants. He knew that sound. It meant her release was right there. If he were fucking her, she'd be squeezing him so tight he'd explode. He rubbed his dick, his fingers toying with his zipper. Fuck, he wanted her but he had so much more planned. He stepped back, his chest heaving. "You are fucking delicious."

CHAPTER 29: MAGGIE

Maggie almost cried when Terry moved from between her legs. Her body was stretched tight with desire and need. He'd teased her before, taking her to the edge and retreating but never like this. Never over and over again. She couldn't take anymore. "Please, Sir."

"Shhh, baby." He moved to stand at her side, brushing the hair from her face. "Trust me. This will be so good." He bent and kissed her, his mouth soothing and gentle, but she needed hot and passionate.

Her arms jerked in the restraints, trying to wrap around his neck, hold him to her. Her tongue danced with his but he kept retreating, keeping the kiss soft and warm. She didn't want to calm down, to back away from passion. The next time his tongue dipped past her lips, she sucked on it, pulling it deep into her mouth and it was like flipping a sex switch. Terry grabbed her head, holding her in place as he thrust into her mouth, his kiss wild and desperate just like she felt. She yanked on her restraints as his hand cupped her breast, pinching her nipple.

"Yes, please, Sir." She needed that and more.

He pulled away, his dark eyes half-lidded with passion. "That's enough." He seemed to be talking more to himself than her. He was close to losing control, to giving her what she wanted.

"Please, Sir. I need to touch you." She wiggled her fingers. "Run my nails down your back, your neck. Stroke your dick."

His nostrils flared and he almost growled as he took a step back. "You're being a naughty rabbit."

"I can be naughtier. Let me touch you." Her eyes dropped to his crotch. "That must be uncomfortable. Squeezed in there so tight." If she got a hold of his cock, it was over. He was already on edge.

"How about a drink?" He turned and walked into the kitchen.

"Damnit, Terry. I'm not thirsty." She wanted sex, not a drink.

He came back with a bottle of water. "Open."

She frowned but obeyed. He put the bottle at her mouth and her eyes locked with his as she wrapped her lips around the opening, sucking and swallowing like it was his cock.

"Enough." His jaw clenched as he pulled the bottle away. "Now a cherry. Whipped cream or chocolate?"

She sighed. She wasn't going to win. "Whipped cream."

He filled a cherry and then offered it to her. "Open."

She did and he dropped it into her mouth. It was tart and delicious – the sweetness of the whipped cream blending perfectly with the tartness of the fruit and the decadence of the fudge.

"Another?" He held up a cherry.

"Yes, please." It was good and she hadn't eaten much at dinner.

He prepared another and gave it to her, watching as she chewed. His dark gaze keeping her insides molten even as her desperation from earlier waned.

"How are you feeling?" He bent, kissing the side of her mouth, his tongue darting out to clean a smidgeon of whipped cream.

"Better…and not." She smiled sheepishly. It was no secret how much she needed him but her eagerness for his touch still made her blush.

"I know this is hard, but it'll be worth it." He kissed her again, his tongue dipping into her mouth before he pulled away. "Trust me?"

"I suppose, I have to." She moved her arms a bit. "Kind of got myself into a situation here."

He laughed. "The right answer is Yes, Sir or always, Sir, but I'll take it." His hand drifted down her check and over her chest to skim along her abdomen. "Time to pay for cherry number three."

CHAPTER 30: MAGGIE

"No. Please, Sir." Maggie couldn't do it again. Her body was calmer now but if Terry took her to the edge again and refused to let her come, she'd scream and cry and she had no idea what else. "Please, Sir, fuck me." She needed him now and when she talked dirty it turned him on – a lot.

"Oh, I will but not yet." His eyes gleamed with both desire and amusement. "First, you have to see your punishment through to the end."

"What are you getting?" Her heart stilled as he walked over to his bag. She couldn't take another toy. She just couldn't but her body didn't agree as more wetness pooled between her legs.

"Guess."

"How can…" The hum of a vibrator filled the room. "No. Oh, god, Terry. No. I can't." She'd lose it. She'd break apart. Combust.

"You can and you will." He walked back to her side. "Take a deep breath."

Her eyes locked with his. Her soul found peace in his

dark, confident gaze but her body trembled with need as he lowered his hand, letting the vibrator skim along her abdomen.

She tensed, her pussy throbbing, needing that tingly touch as he trailed it up her thigh and back down. Her breath froze each time the toy neared her pussy and then she exhaled almost in tears as he slid it down her thigh, away from where she needed it. "Please," she whimpered, begging for that touch. She closed her eyes as the vibrations tickled along her flesh, drawing closer and closer until..."Oh. Yes." Her eyes flew open and she gasped as pulsations shot through her. She arched toward the toy, trying to make him touch her harder but he only skimmed it over her pussy lips.

"What do you want, rabbit? I see you trying to move. Tell me what you want."

"Oh…Sir…please. More. Harder." Her voice was so raw with need she barely recognized it.

"Like this?" He held the vibrator against her pussy and she moaned low and loud, closing her eyes as the sensations raced through her. Her hips rocked as she reached for her orgasm. It was right there. All she needed was another moment, another touch.

"Not yet." He pulled the toy away, turning it off.

She sobbed, tears of frustration streaming down her cheeks.

"Shhh." He kissed her. "Almost, rabbit."

CHAPTER 31: TERRY

Terry picked up another cherry. Maggie was so close to coming a stray breeze would probably push her over the edge. He filled it with liqueur.

"No. Please. I can't." Her gaze was unfocused, still partially lost to her passion.

"Hold still. You don't want to drop anymore, do you?"

"No. Sir. Please."

"Don't worry. They're not very cold anymore." He placed it on the top of her breast.

Her breathing slowed as she tried to keep it steady but her body was a mess of desire and frustration. The cherry wobbled. "I can't."

He put a finger on it, holding it in place while he grabbed another one and placed it on her other breast. "Concentrate, rabbit." He moved his hands, grabbing the chocolate liqueur and pouring it into the second cherry. His lips turned up in a smirk as he overfilled it, watching as the dark liquid ran down her pale skin.

"Sir. No." The cherries rolled off her chest. She

sobbed. "I can't. I can't take any more."

He shook his head. "You really made a mess, rabbit. I'm going to have to clean you up again." He grabbed the can of whipped cream.

"What are you going to do with that?" There was a hint of panic in her tone.

"You know I like whipped cream with my chocolate." He sprayed the cream around her nipples.

"That's cold." She wiggled, making her gorgeous breasts sway.

He couldn't wait any longer to taste them. He lowered his head, not even bothering to lick and tease, but latching right onto her breast and devouring the whipped cream and her flesh. Her nipple, already hard, grew harder in his mouth as she writhed beneath him, testing her restraints.

He kissed his way to her other breast, taking his time with this one, teasing as he lapped at the whipped cream.

"Please…" Her arms yanked on the restraints but he'd hooked them good and tight.

He finished cleaning the whipped cream and moved down the sides of her breast, mumbling, "Gotta get all the chocolate." He sucked the side of her breast, making her moan and then blew across her nipple as he made his way to the other side.

"Sir…please." She was so close to coming, her body was tight as a bow.

He had to be inside her. He had to feel it when she broke apart when she shattered on the cliff of passion he'd created. He pulled her nipple into his mouth, sucking hard as he undid his pants, pushing them and his underwear down. He stepped out of them and straightened

"Don't stop. Please, don't stop," she almost sobbed.

"I'll be back."

"No, please," she begged and then clamped her mouth shut as he stepped between her legs.

"It's time, rabbit." He rubbed his cock along her wet heat. She was soaked and swollen, more than ready.

"May I come?" Her eyes widened with hope as her chest heaved, making her large breasts jiggle.

"Yes. Let's count the times."

CHAPTER 32: MAGGIE

"No. Ple…" Maggie's words turned into a moan as Terry's cock slid inside her. Her body clenched around him. This was what she needed.

"That's it, rabbit." He pulled almost all the way out and then pushed back inside, his dark eyes locked with hers. "Fuck, you feel so good."

Her hands fisted as he pumped into her in long, hard thrusts. She needed to cling to him, to feel his heat under her fingertips. "Sir, please. I need to touch you."

"Not this time." He hooked his finger through the O-ring and pulled up her head. "Look." His gaze dropped to where his dick slid in and out of her.

His cock was so big and yet, her body craved every inch—clamping onto him as he entered her, never wanting him to leave. He thrust faster, his motions strong and purposeful. She needed this. She needed him and although he wasn't close to release, she could feel that edge. Lightning shot through her body from where they were connected, turning her into nothing but sparks. She moaned as he bent, his mouth capturing her nipple, his teeth scraping across her sensitive bud. Her pussy tightened around his thick cock as he bit down just enough to send a sizzle of pain bursting through the pleasure and she screamed. Her back arched as her body tightened, trembling beneath him as she came. He stilled, his chest heaving, letting her ride out her orgasm on his dick.

"Come back to me, rabbit." He brushed some hair from her face as he pulled from her body. "We aren't done yet."

"No. Please." She was spent. Exhausted. She wanted to curl in his arms and sleep.

"Again." He strode into the kitchen and came back a moment later holding a few cherries. "I saved these. Wanted to make sure they were nice and cold. I remember how much you enjoyed it last time." He dropped them on the table before popping one in his mouth and holding it between his teeth.

Her heart threatened to thud from her chest as his dark head lowered between her legs.

He pulled the cherry from his mouth, spreading her lower lips. "Fuck, you're luscious."

She leaned up, twitching as he rolled the frozen cherry along her leg.

"Too cold?" His eyes gleamed.

"Yes." She almost panted. She wanted his mouth on her. She needed the biting cold of the cherry and the heat of his tongue.

"Let me warm it up." He put it in his mouth and slowly

lowered his face, his hot breath teasing across her aching flesh.

"Oh….please, Sir." Her eyes grew heavy but she kept them open. He was so large and strong, all male between her legs.

His tongue came out licking along her crease, the cherry rolling along with it. Sensations both hot and cold exploded on her aching flesh.

"Oh…" She moaned as he held the cherry to the side, his tongue dipping into her body.

He opened her wider, rolling the cherry upward over the outer lips of her pussy.

She tensed. It was still so cold. "Sir…no. I can't…"

He rolled the cherry over her clit and she shook as waves of shock from the cold roared through her. He rolled it back and forth and then his mouth was there, hot and wet, taking away the cold, sucking before his tongue teased her clit. She fell over the edge, screaming as she came again, her body shaking and her hips undulating against his face.

This time when she opened her eyes, he was standing at her side, his dark eyes hot and heavy with desire. "Again, rabbit."

"No." She shook her head. She was boneless. Beyond exhausted. "I can't. I mean it. I really can't."

"You can." He turned on the vibrator and her body trembled, both in dread and anticipation.

"Sir. No. I'll…" Her words froze as he placed the toy against her pussy. She yanked at her restraints, trying to get away from the pain-pleasure of the vibrations ricocheting against her over-sensitized flesh.

"You were saying?" He rubbed the toy, along her clit, pressing down and she almost sat up, her arms and legs pulling on the restraint. "Don't fight it, rabbit."

"Oh...oh..." She had no words, nothing but waves of pleasure pulling her under into bliss.

He pressed a lever and raised the St. Andrew's Cross until she was upright again. He rubbed the vibrator along her pussy as he leaned over and pulled another one from his bag. This one was slim and long. He dropped the first toy to the side as he slid the thin one inside her.

She gasped as he pumped it into her, in and out. The vibrations were great but it was too thin and cool. She wanted his cock—hard, hot and big.

"Ready, rabbit?" He stroked his dick, sliding the tip against her clit.

"Yes. Please."

"Good." He removed the toy, turning it off as he slid inside her.

"Yes." This is what she'd wanted—him inside her.

"You like that?" He rocked a little. "You like my giant cock, don't you?"

"Yes." She shifted her hips, taking him deeper and his nostrils flared.

"You're gonna have both your holes filled." He slid the vibrator between her butt cheeks, the tip teasing along her hole.

"Oh...yes. Please." She tensed, waiting for him to turn

it on and for those vibrations to fill her.

"Relax." He bent, taking her nipple in his mouth and teasing with his tongue and teeth.

She tried to reach for him, but instead her fingers clenched air and her chest heaved as he slipped the toy deeper inside her butthole.

He lifted his head. "You good?"

"Yes. God, yes." She was better than good. She needed him to move, to thrust, to fuck her until she was nothing but feeling.

"What do you want, rabbit?"

"Fuck me, sir. Please."

He grabbed her O-ring pulling her head to his and he kissed her. It was wild and desperate, his hips thrusting into her over and over. This time he was close. The games were done. He fucked her harder and faster, the feelings of pleasure merging together and slipping from her lips as one long moan. His face dropped to the side of her neck, his breath coming in pants as he pumped into her. His fingers moved between her legs and the vibrator came to life. The sensations shot through her body, intensifying the feel of his cock stroking into her. He must've felt them too or maybe it was how hard she clamped down on him because he groaned in her ear and his dick seemed to grow as he lost all rhythm and control. He fucked her like a madman, each thrust making her clench around both him and the toy in her ass.

He pumped into her again, hitting that spot and

sending her spiraling off the cliff. She screamed, her body tightening and shaking. He grabbed her hips, holding her still. The toy pulsed in her ass as he thrust into her again and again, pushing her through her release and into another one. Her mouth opened but no sound came out. She was lost. Breathless. She shattered into a million tiny sparks of pleasure. He stiffened and shouted, his body freezing for a moment as he came, and then his hips moved slower and slower, emptying himself inside her.

He collapsed onto her. "I never want to move," he said against her neck. "I'm going to stay like this, buried deep inside you forever."

"Sounds good to me but untie me first so I can touch you."

He smiled against her skin. "That means I have to move, but for you, anything." He reached up, unlatching her hands. She clung to him, her fingers skimming across his hot, silky skin a moment before her arms tightened, clinging to him—this man she loved and who loved her—for now and forever.

CHAPTER 33: TERRY

Terry crawled into bed next to Maggie, pulling her into his arms. She curled against him, soft and warm. His. His love.

His heart raced and his gut clenched with fear. This was a disaster and yet, he was truly happy for the first time in years. After his divorce, once he'd adjusted to his new life without the kids around all the time, he'd become content. Building his new law practice had kept him extraordinarily busy and at night he'd had his friends and the Club. He hadn't even realized that he'd been missing something. He kissed her head, her hair still damp from the shower. The words tangled in his throat for a moment but he forced them out. "I love you."

She leaned up; her hazel eyes filled with love. "I love you too." She kissed him. It was soft and gentle. A kiss of care and comfort, companionship and love, not sex. "When did you know?"

Shit. Here came the two thousand questions. He

110

sighed. "I don't know, Maggie."

"You have to have some idea." She snuggled closer to him.

"I don't know when I fell in love with you but I realized it right before you called me on Friday."

"Friday?" She leaned up, slapping his chest. "You've known for over twenty-four hours and you just now told me?"

"Yes." He tugged on her collar, pulling her back into his arms. "And this wasn't exactly how I wanted to do it."

"What do you mean?" She leaned on his chest, staring at him.

"I wanted it to be perfect but then...well, we fought and...you know the rest."

"Terry, it was perfect." She kissed him.

"Hardly. It was probably the worst confession of love ever."

"I don't know. Telling me I've ruined you for other women is pretty romantic to me." She grinned and he swore his heart actually melted.

"Let's not mention that to anyone."

"Oh. I wanted to tell Sarah and Annie."

"You'd better not." He swatted her ass. "Or you'll pay."

"Promise?" She grinned and snuggled under his arm.

"Absolutely." He kissed her head. "Thank you for this weekend." He rolled to his side, scooting down so he could look her in the eyes. "Did you like it? What we did? Being here?" This was important. She was the most giving Sub he'd ever been with and that meant he had to be the best Dom he'd ever been. He had to ferret out her feelings so he could take care of her. "Tell me the truth. If you don't want to come back, we don't have—"

"You'd better bring me back." She touched his face. "I loved everything about this weekend. I love you. I want to do this with you."

He swallowed. "Only if you're sure, Maggie. I just…" His eyes dropped. This was so hard to say.

"What?" She ran her hand up his chest. "You can tell me anything. Whatever you want to do…I'll try."

"No. That's not it." His gaze darted to hers. "That's not what I was going to say."

"Then what were you—"

"That I can give this up. I can give up anything but you." His arms tightened around her. "I don't love easily. I never thought I'd love again but now that I have….I can't…I can't lose you." He'd never survive if she left him. He'd barely survived last time and this love was so much more. He was older. He appreciated how rare a gift like this was.

"Oh Terry." She kissed him again. "I'm not going anywhere. I swear."

"Promise that if I ever do something that pisses you off, you'll tell me. We'll talk. We won't let it get bad."

"I promise." She kissed him again. "I'm not the same woman you met. I'm not going to sit quietly by as this…our relationship dies. I'll do whatever I can to keep

112

you here. With me."

"Here?" He smiled, pulling her closer. "As in here in bed? Or here in the Club? Or maybe you want to keep me here." He ran his finger along her pussy.

"The first one yes. The second sometimes."

"And the third?" He slipped the tip of his finger inside her.

"And the third one"—her breath hitched in her chest as he slid his finger in farther—"always, even though I think you're trying to kill me."

"I guess I should stop then." He teased her clit with his thumb.

"Don't you dare." She grabbed his hand, keeping it between her legs. "You started it. You need to finish it."

"As you wish, rabbit." He thrust two fingers inside her as he pushed her to her back for one more fuck before he passed out.

Thanks for reading His Love.
I hope you enjoyed the story.

If you missed Terry and Maggie's first night at the Club, you can find it on my website www.EllisODay.com

Or go straight to the retailers.

https://books2read.com/u/4XZPN9

Looking for more of the delicious stories about the men

and women of La Petite Mort Club? Check out the excerpts coming up next.

Playing House. This story is all about Nick and Sarah's weekend watching Maggie's kids.

His Sub — How Maggie and Terry meet.

Interviewing for her Lover — Nick and Sarah's first, kinky night together.

The Voyeur–When Patrick catches Annie watching a couple have sex and the sparks ignite.

Plus, if you sign up for my newsletter, you can get the entire Six Nights of Sin series for free (all six nights of Nick and Sarah's contract—every delicious fantasy) as a thank you gift.

Go to my website or email me for details:

www.EllisODay.com

authorellisoday@gmail.com

Playing House

Sarah grabbed the takeout and grocery bags from her car and walked into the house. "Hey, boys. Can't pet you. Got my hands full here." She tried to push past her two dogs, but that was no easy feat. Tank was a Belgian Malinois, a retired military dog, and Sweetie was a pit-bull mix. One of them alone could block the doorway but both together, wiggling and wagging their tails could push her back into the garage.

"You need help?" hollered Nick from the living room.

"No. I got it." She squeezed between the two monsters and opened the laundry room door, stepping into the main part of the house.

Nick sat on the couch, glancing up from his laptop. "Wow. You got a lot of food. Want some help putting it away."

"No. Thanks." She headed into the kitchen. She was the luckiest woman alive. Not only was he gorgeous— black hair, brown eyes and a body she drooled over—but he was the most helpful man she'd ever met, never skimping on doing more than his share of housework.

She dropped everything on the counter and began putting away the groceries. She slipped the dessert she'd gotten from her friend, Maggie, in the back of the refrigerator. She couldn't have him chowing down on it now. She may need that sugary safety net to assuage his temper after she told him she'd volunteered them to watch Maggie's three children this weekend.

Nick loved kids. He probably wouldn't mind babysitting but she should've asked him first. It'd been a spur of the moment thing and Maggie had been so excited. She couldn't back out now. She grabbed the takeout bags, opening the premade salad and dumping it into a bowl. "You ready to eat?"

"Always," he answered.

She jumped, her heart pounding. "You scared me."

"I see that." Nick stood in the doorway, looking sexy as always—hair a little too long and mussed, dark eyes roaming over her. His worn jeans hugged his body, letting her know that he was semi-aroused and making her heart race for an entirely different reason than surprise.

Would she ever quit turning into a quivering mess of desire when he looked at her? She hoped not, but she didn't have to let him know how he affected her. It was good for him to have to work for it. "I got salad and Thai food."

"Salad and Thai food? What kind of combination is that?"

"Salad is good for us and Thai…that sounded good to me. Since you wouldn't tell me what you were hungry for when I called..." As soon as the words left her lips, she knew her mistake and her blood began to hum in anticipation.

"Oh, you know what I'm hungry for." He prowled closer. "What I'm always hungry for."

She moved to the other side of the table. They both knew how this would end but the game was always fun. "I meant to eat."

"Me too." His grin widened and his eyes darkened as they rested on the juncture between her thighs.

"For dinner. Eat for dinner." Suddenly, she wasn't so hungry.

"Dinner can wait." He stalked her.

Get your copy and find out what happens next.

https://books2read.com/u/4DykXk

His Sub

Terry wandered through the crowd of well-dressed women and men at La Petite Mort Club. It was the same scene every time Ethan, his friend and owner of the Club, threw one of these events. The members mingled with the newbies, hoping to snag something different or someone interesting.

Ethan strolled casually toward him, a ready smile on his face as he greeted his guests. "Terry, about time you made it down here."

"Like you can talk." His friend spent most of his time in the back office, watching the Club on monitors.

"I've been mingling for over an hour."

"It's your business not mine." He leaned against the balustrade, peering down on the crowd.

"True, but you could sell your practice and buy me out."

"And run this place?" He laughed. "No thank you." He tossed back his scotch. "I spend enough time here as it is." He used to practically live here except when he was at the office or in court, but lately he'd been staying home more.

"Good turn out tonight." Ethan waved at a waitress and a moment later they each had another drink.

"Yeah, but I don't see one interesting person in this crop of wannabe members."

"And you can tell if someone is interesting just by looking at them?"

"I can tell not one of them has an original thought. Look at them. They're all in red." The Club was awash in a sea of red dresses—short, long, dark, light but always red.

"It is a Valentine's Day party."

"I know but you'd think one woman"—he held up his finger—"one would consider that everyone else would be in red and wear a different color."

"There are some pinks out there."

"Same thing, just lighter."

Ethan grabbed his phone from his pocket and looked at the text, frowning.

"Problem?" The Club was usually a safe place but on open night events, when Ethan allowed non-members access in order to recruit new members, the place could get dangerous.

"A little skirmish over a woman." Ethan grinned, his blue eyes sparkling as a couple of young guys hurried past them, almost tripping in their haste to stay close to a group of very attractive women. "These youngsters haven't learned that sharing is more fun."

He ignored Ethan's teasing. He'd taken a lot of shit from Ethan, Nick and even Patrick because he wasn't into the sharing thing. He preferred it to be him and one woman, one sweet, little sub. Since he was in no mood to listen to any more crap, he'd change the subject. "Those kids barely look old enough to drink."

"You're showing your age." Ethan patted his shoulder. "You should find some nice, young thing and teach her how to please her master."

"Maybe I will, if any of them show enough originality to dress in something other than red."

"I've got to go and sort out this problem." Ethan slid his phone into his pocket. "I'll find you later. If you find that elusive non-red dress, I'd suggest we share but..." He chuckled as he headed down the stairs, maneuvering through the crowd like he had nowhere to go, when in reality he was heading for the back—the playrooms.

Terry's eyes stopped and lingered on the new hire, Desiree, who was moving around the room, talking and flirting with all the men and some women. She was interesting—exotic and smart—but there was a shrewdness behind her eyes that he'd learned a long time ago to avoid. A woman like her had an agenda and she stuck with it, no matter what.

Someone slammed into his back, causing his drink to spill down his front, staining his shirt and suit.

"Oh…oh, I'm so sorry."

He spun around and encountered a red dress and breasts—milky white and lush. The skin would be fragrant and softer than rose petals.

"Oh. Your shirt. Let me get something to wipe that up."

He forced his eyes away from those lovely breasts. Her hair was a rich mahogany. It'd probably hang past her shoulders in waves of curly silk but right now it was piled haphazardly on her head in what had been some kind of elegant style before disobedient strands had escaped their restraint. She looked mussed and damnit, he wanted to be the one to muss her.

"Paper towels? Napkins?" She glanced around and then hurried over to the bar.

She was short and curvy—her body succulent, ripe and he'd bet juicy. She grabbed a stack of napkins and headed for him. Her dress was too tight, like she'd recently gained some weight. He usually went for the tall, athletic types but for some reason his dick had picked this woman.

She returned to his side and dabbed at the wetness on his shirt and jacket as if she actually gave a shit about his clothes. This was no subtle caress, no flirtation—just indifferent efficiency.

"I'm so sorry." She wadded the napkins in her hand, still patting at his clothes.

"You said that already." His words came out gruffer than he'd meant. No one treated him with disinterest. He was a rich, successful, attractive man and she was treating him like a child. He wanted to pull up her—unfortunately, red—dress and fuck her right here. They were at the Club. It wasn't out of the question.

Her hand froze. "Oh." Her large hazel eyes looked startled and then hurt. "Sorry. Ah, excuse me." She headed toward the stairs, dropping the wet napkins in the trash before disappearing in the crowd.

He turned around, so he could see the first floor and waited for her to appear. She hurried across the downstairs room, bumping and stumbling through the crowd. A lone, scared, little rabbit in a room full of predators. She stopped for a moment, scanning the crowd as if searching for someone.

"Who are you looking for, little rabbit?" he mumbled to himself. "A husband? Boyfriend?" He grinned as he lifted his scotch to his lips. "Girlfriend?" He frowned at the empty glass. "You spilled my drink. I'll forgive you, but it's going to cost you." He waved at one of the waitresses. "Everything has a price, little rabbit." As one of the best divorce lawyers in town, he knew that better than anyone.

The waitress brought him another drink. He paid,

giving her a large tip before turning to find his little rabbit. He took a sip of the scotch, enjoying the smooth burn and his lush little bunny's journey through La Petite Mort Club. She froze in her tracks, her jaw dropping open as she gazed at a threesome on one of the couches.

The woman was sandwiched between two men, stroking one's cock as the other man fondled her beneath her red dress. The man behind her looked up and said something to the little rabbit. Her face heated and Terry's eyes dropped to her chest. Yep, they were a pretty shade of pink but what he really wanted to know was if the color matched her pussy.

She stumbled away from the threesome, bumping into another man. It was Richard, who stopped her from falling and then immediately let her go, stepping away. She was safe with Richard. As a member of the Club and a gentleman, he knew that safewords were law and consent was absolutely necessary. She said something to Richard and continued through the Club, disappearing in the crowd.

"You're not getting away that easily." He followed along on the upper floor, keeping her in sight. He had no idea why but he wanted her. Maybe it was simply because she was different than everyone else here.

He took another sip of his drink. It was obviously the little rabbit's first time at a place like this but she didn't seem eager to participate or interested in watching. She truly seemed to be looking for someone specific—not just someone to fuck. Well, she'd found the latter because he was going to fuck her. In the office he followed his head but at La Petite Mort Club his cock was king.

She headed toward the playrooms. There was no way he was going to miss this. He sauntered down the stairs, grabbing another drink on the way. She wasn't hard to follow. She left a path of irritated people in her wake as she bumped into them and apologized profusely before hurrying forward. Her full, round hips swayed under her tight, red dress that'd seen better days—hem frayed and at least five years out of style. Not that he minded, especially the snug fit of the cloth, but his women were usually much more put tougher.

They were the CEO types—women who thrived on being in charge. He enjoyed teaching them how much fun turning over control could be. When they were with him, he was their dom, their master and he made sure they loved every second. He told them when to kneel, when to suck, when to spread their legs or ass and when to come. The more power they had in their everyday life the more they craved bowing to his wishes. His little rabbit wouldn't know what power was. She was a hot mess of a woman. Still, his dick wanted her, so his dick would have her.

She was hurrying out of the first playroom when he entered the hallway. Her eyes were huge and her cheeks were on fire. She ducked into the next room and quickly came out—even redder than before.

"Excuse me." He'd offer his assistance in her search. She'd be grateful. He could capitalize on that unless she was looking for her husband or boyfriend. He wasn't in the mood to share. He would, however, allow the other man to watch. He could give the guy some pointers on how to take care of his wife because this woman obviously needed guidance.

"You?" Her eyes narrowed.

That wasn't the reaction he was used to. Women usually purred for him.

"Are you following me?"

"What would you do if I said I was?" He took a step toward her.

"I'd scream. There are bouncers here. I saw them."

Lord, she was cute. "Yes, but if they came running at every little scream they'd die of exhaustion."

As if to emphasis his point a woman screamed in ecstasy. His little rabbit's face heated and she averted her gaze.

"Who are you looking for?" He ran his finger lightly down her cheek. Her skin was as smooth as porcelain but much warmer and softer.

"Ah..." Her breath hitched, making her breasts swell dangerously above her gown.

He could have her out of it in a minute. The skin would be even softer than that on her face. "Did you lose your husband?"

"No." She licked her lips.

There was no way he could let that offer pass. He slowly bent, giving her time to refuse him. He may command his women but he made sure they always wanted it first. Her eyes dropped to his mouth and he couldn't help a slight smirk. She wanted this as much as he did. He moved closer and let his lips rest gently on hers. He'd take it slow, make her yearn for him and then he'd make her obey.

"What are you doing?" She turned her head.

"Kissing you." His lips brushed against her cheek. He wasn't about to lose ground.

"Why?" She turned again, her eyes meeting his.

The confusion in her hazel gaze was as obvious as the hideous dress on her gorgeous body. She may remind him of a rabbit but she couldn't be that naive. She had to be in her mid to late thirties.

He should use flowery words—tell her she was beautiful, desirable—but that wasn't him. Blunt was the kindest word to describe him. "Because, I want to."

"You don't even know me."

He was losing ground. The interest in her face was being replaced with disgust. "No, but I know I want you." Damn, he shouldn't have said that.

"Well, too bad." She pushed on his chest and he stepped back, letting her pass.

"This is a sex club, you know." He followed. "If you aren't here for sex, why are you here?"

She spun around. "I'm quite aware of what this place is and just because I don't want you, a stranger to...to"—she waved her hand about—"in the hallway."

He laughed. "We wouldn't be the first. There are people fucking in the main room."

"I know. I saw." Her cheeks heated.

He stepped closer. "You are adorable." He touched a strand of hair that was resting on her shoulder. It was like satin.

"I'm a mess." She pulled her hair free from his fingers.

"A hot mess. A fiery, hot, sexy mess." He moved closer with every other word. "One I want to fuck, right now."

Her eyes hardened. "Too bad because I don't"—again she waved her hand about—"you know, with strangers in the hallway." She shoved his chest again.

He took a small step back but he wasn't giving up yet. "We can go to a private room."

"No."

Shit. By the look on her face, he'd just made a bigger blunder.

"Let me go." She pushed him again.

Damn. She'd said the worst three words in the English language besides I love you. He moved away, releasing her for the moment. "Sorry."

She harrumphed.

"I made a mistake."

"Yes, you did." She hurried down the hallway but not before he'd seen the look of hurt in her large eyes.

"What the fuck do you want from me? I made a mistake and apologized." He trailed after her.

"I want you to leave me alone. Please. Go away."

He stopped. His little rabbit was running but perhaps, he shouldn't chase. She darted down a hallway toward the hardcore BDSM rooms.

Normally, she'd be fine—embarrassed but fine. Except with all the newbies here, tonight wasn't a normal night. He hurried after her. "Hey, I don't think you want to go—"

"Leave me alone." She walked faster. "I need to find my friend and get out of here."

"Okay, but I don't—"

"Go away." She sounded both mad and as if she were going to cry.

"Suit yourself, but I warned you."

She strode into the closest room. He should leave. Let her find out that he wasn't the worst thing in a place like this, not in a long shot, but his feet followed her. She was his little rabbit. He'd found her. No one else was going to enjoy her until he'd had his taste.

"Vicky? Vicky? Are you in here?"

He stepped into the room, staying in the shadows. She was looking around in the dark for her friend. It only took a moment for one of the six guys to notice the little rabbit who'd stumbled into their den.

"Shit," he mumbled. Not one of those guys was a regular.

Grab your free copy and find out what happens next.

ELLIS O. DAY

LA PETITE MORT CLUB

INTERVIEWING
FOR HER LOVER

SIX NIGHTS OF SIN SERIES

Free: Interviewing For Her Lover

"Do I have to take off my clothes?" Sarah tugged on the hem of her black dress. It was shorter and lower cut in the front than she normally wore, but the Viewing was about finding a man for sex and according to Ethan men liked to look.

"No." Ethan turned her away from the door and forced her to look at him. "You don't have to do anything you don't want to do."

She stared into his blue eyes. Why couldn't he be interested in her? She'd only met with him five or six times, but she trusted him. He ran his business, La Petite Mort Club, very professionally and he was gorgeous with his sandy brown hair, strong cheekbones and vibrant blue eyes. Sex between them would be good. Easy. He was attractive and...not for her. She didn't want decent sex or good sex, she wanted mind blowing, screaming orgasms and that wouldn't happen between him and her because there was no chemistry, no attraction.

"Listen to me." He moved his hands to her shoulders and gave her a gentle shake. "You aren't selling yourself to the highest bidder. You're looking for a partner. One who'll"—he grinned—"turn you on in ways you can't even imagine."

She glanced at the door where the men waited. Waited for her. Waited to decide if they wanted to fuck her. "I'm a bit nervous."

"About what?"

This was embarrassing, but she'd been honest with him up to this point. She'd had to be. He was helping her...had helped her to choose the five men in the other room. "What if none of them..."

"They will want you." He touched her chin, turning her face toward him. "A few of them may back out after this but not because they don't want you."

"Yeah, right."

"I'm only going to say this once. You're beautiful and

different, unique."

"That's not necessarily a good thing." She had long legs and a nice body—trim and firm—but with her auburn hair and green eyes she was cute at best, not gorgeous. The men she'd chosen were all rich, good looking and powerful. They could have anyone they wanted.

"It's exactly what they want, or most of them anyway." He took her hand and led her closer to the door.

She leaned on his arm, hating these shoes. She should've stuck with her flats but Ethan had given her a list of what she should wear and high heels were on the top. She'd found the smallest heels in the store and by Ethan's look when he'd first seen her she might've been better off going barefoot. He'd met her at the private entrance and his gaze had been appreciating as it'd skimmed over her dress until he got to her feet. Then he'd frowned and shook his head.

"Finding the right men for you wasn't easy." He stopped at the door.

"Thanks a lot." She shifted away from him, his words hurting a little. She hadn't been sure of her appeal to the opposite sex in a long time, not since the early years with Adam.

"It's not because you aren't beautiful but because you want to be dominated and you want to dominate—"

"I do not want to dominate." All she could picture was a woman in black leather with a whip and that wasn't her, not at all.

"If you say so." He smiled a little. "But, you do want

to lead the scene. Right? Because that's what—"

"Yes." Her face was red. She could feel it. She didn't want to talk about her fantasies again. It'd been embarrassing enough the first time, but he'd had to know what she wanted to compile a list of candidates.

"Most at the club are either doms or subs. Very few are switches." His eyes raked over her. "That's what's so special about you. You want it all and…that's what made choosing these men difficult."

He'd given her a selection of twenty-two men who might be interested in what she wanted. She'd narrowed it down to seven. Two had been uninterested when he'd approached. That'd left her with the five who'd see her in person for the first time tonight, but she wouldn't see them. That'd come after the Viewing when she interviewed any who were still interested.

"Remember what you want. This is your deal. You call the shots. At least a little." He kissed her forehead. "But don't refuse to give them anything. You don't want a submissive."

"No." That didn't turn her on at all and she only had eight weeks. One night each week for two months before she'd go back to her lonely life, her lonely bed, dreaming of Adam.

"You can do this." He pulled a flask from his jacket and unscrewed the lid. "For courage."

"Thanks." She took a large swallow, the brandy too thick and sweet for her taste but it was better than nothing.

"Now, go find your lover."

She laughed a little but sadness swept through her. There'd be no love between this man and herself. This would be sex, fucking. That's all. The only man she'd ever love, her only lover, was dead. This was purely physical. "Thank you again." She stood on tip-toe and kissed his cheek. He may be gorgeous and run a sex club but he was a good man, a good friend.

She turned and opened the door and walked into the room, trying to stay balanced on these stupid heels. Men wouldn't find them so attractive if they had to wear them. The room was dark except for one light highlighting a small platform. That was for her. She stepped up onto the small stage. The room was silent but they were there, above her, hidden behind the one-way mirrors, watching and deciding if they wanted to take the next step—to eventually take her.

She stared into the blackness of the room. It wasn't huge but its emptiness made it seem vast. She glanced upward, the light making her squint and she quickly stared back into the darkness. This was arranged for them to see her. That was it. She'd get no glimpse of them yet. She'd seen their pictures, chosen them but meeting them in person would be different. A picture couldn't tell her their smell or the sound of their voices.

She tugged at her dress where it hugged her hips, wishing the questions would start, but there was only silence. She shifted, the heels already killing her feet. Ethan hadn't liked them and if they weren't going to impress, she might as well take them off. She moved to the back of the stage, leaned against the wall and removed her shoes. As she returned to the center of the stage a man spoke, his voice loud and commanding almost echoing throughout the room.

"Don't stop there. Take off your dress."

She bent, placing her shoes on the floor. That wasn't part of the deal. She wasn't going to undress in front of five men, only one. Only the one she chose. She straightened. "No."

"What?" He was surprised and not happy.

"I said no. That's not part of the Viewing."

"I want to see what I'm getting."

She stared up toward the windows, squinting a little. She couldn't tell from where the voice had come. The speaker system made it sound as if it were coming from God himself. "And you will if I pick you."

Another man laughed.

"It's not funny. She's disobedient," said the man with the loud voice.

"Not always. I can be obedient." These men liked to be in control but sometimes, so did she.

"Will you raise your dress? Just a little," asked another voice.

"Didn't you see enough in the photos?" She'd applied a few months ago for this one-time contract. She'd been excited and nervous when she'd received the acceptance email with an appointment for a photography session.

She'd never had her picture professionally taken, since she didn't count school portraits or the ones her parents had had done at JCPenny's. She'd been anxious and a little turned on imaging wearing her new lingerie in front of a strange man, so she'd been disappointed to find the photographer was an elderly woman, but the lady had put her at ease and the photos had turned out better than she'd expected. She glanced up at the mirrors, hoping she wasn't disappointing all the men. That'd be too embarrassing.

"Those were...nice, but I'd like to see the real thing before deciding if you're worth my time."

She raised a brow. "You can always leave." She shouldn't antagonize him. She was sure the bossy man had already decided against committing to this agreement. Disobedience didn't appeal to him. That left four. If she didn't pick any of them, she could go through the process again, but she didn't think she would.

The man chuckled slightly. "I know that, but I haven't decided I don't want to fuck you. Not yet, anyway."

The word, so harsh and vulgar excited her. It was the truth. That was what she, what they were all deciding. Who'd get to fuck her. It was what she wanted, what she'd agreed to do, and as much as she dreaded it, she wanted it. She was tired of being alone. She missed having a man inside her—his tongue and fingers and cock.

"Do any of you have any questions?" She clasped her dress at her waist and slowly gathered it upward, displaying more and more of her long legs. She ran. They were in shape. The men would like them.

"Lower your top," said the same man who'd told her to take off her dress.

She didn't like him. If he didn't back out, she'd have Ethan remove him from her list. He was too commanding. He'd never allow her to be in control.

"I don't know if he's done looking at my legs yet." She continued raising the dress until her black and green lace panties were almost exposed.

"Very nice and thank you," said the polite man.

"You're welcome." This man might work. She shifted the dress up another inch before dropping it, giving them a glance at her panties.

"Now, your top," said the bossy guy.

She lowered her spaghetti string off one shoulder, letting the dress dip, but not enough to show anything besides the side of her bra.

"More," he said.

"No." She raised the strap, covering herself. She didn't like this man and wished he'd leave. She'd kick him out but that wasn't part of the process and they were very firm about their rules at this club.

"He got to see your pussy. Why don't I get to see your tits?"

"You got to see as much as he did." She was ready to move on. She bent and picked up her shoes. "If there's nothing else, gentleman, we can set up times for the interview process."

"Turn around," said another man.

It was a command, but she didn't mind. There was a politeness to his order and something about the texture of his voice caused an ache between her thighs. There was a caress in his tone but with an edge and a promise of a good hard fuck.

"Are you going to obey?" His words were whisper soft and smooth.

"Yes." That was going to be part of this too. Her commanding and him commanding. She dropped her shoes and turned.

"Raise you dress again."

She looked over her shoulder at where she imagined he sat watching her.

"Please." There was humor in his tone.

She smiled and slowly gathered the dress upward. She stopped right below the curve of her bottom.

"More. Please." There was a little less humor in his voice.

She wanted to show him her ass. She wanted to show that voice everything but not with the others around. This would be just her and one man, one stranger. That was one of her rules. "No. Only if you're picked do you get to see any more of me than you have." She dropped her dress, grabbed her shoes and walked off the stage and out the door.

She was going to have sex with a stranger. She was going to live out her fantasies for eight nights with a man she didn't know and would never really know, but she wasn't going to lose who she was. She'd keep her honor and her dignity which meant she had to pick a man who'd agree with her rules.

Get your free copy and find out what happens next.

http://myBook.to/SixNSin_Book1

Free: The Voyeur

Annie finished making the bed and gathered the sheets from the floor, keeping them as far away from her body as possible. These sex rooms were disgusting and Ethan was a jerk making her work as a maid. She almost had her Bachelor's Degree in Culinary Arts, but he'd refused to hire her for the kitchen—too many men in the kitchen. The only job he'd give her at La Petite Mort Club was as a maid and unfortunately, she needed the money too badly to refuse.

She stuffed the dirty sheets into the cart and hurried out the door. She had almost thirty minutes before she had to be at the next "sex room." She hid the cart in a closet and darted down a back hallway, staying clear of the cameras. Julie, the woman who supervised the daytime maids, was a real bitch. If she were caught sneaking away from her duties, she'd be assigned to the orgy rooms every day. Right now, they all took turns cleaning that nightmare. She swore they should get hazard pay to even go in those rooms.

She slipped through a doorway and hurried to the one-way mirror. She stared at the couple in the next room. From her first day here, she'd been curious about the activities at the club. She was twenty-four and wasn't a virgin but she'd never, ever done some of these things.

The woman in the room below was tied to a table, legs spread and wearing some sort of leather outfit that left her large breasts free and her crotch exposed. She had shaved her pussy and her pink lower lips were swollen and glistening from her excitement. The man strolled around the table as if he had all night. He still had his pants on but had removed his shirt. His arms and chest were well defined but he had a slight paunch. His erection tented his pants and Annie felt wetness pool between her legs. She had no idea why watching this turned her on but it did.

Ever since she'd accidentally barged in on that guy and girl in the Interview room, she couldn't stop watching.

The man below ran his hand up the woman's inner thigh, glancing over her pussy. The woman thrust her hips upward and Annie ran her own hand between her legs. The man's mouth moved but Annie couldn't hear anything and then he slapped the woman across the thigh hard enough to leave a red mark. Annie jumped. She wasn't into that, but she couldn't stop watching the woman's face. At first, it'd contorted in pain but then it'd morphed into pleasure. The man hit her again and then bent, kissing the red welts—running his tongue across them as his fingers squeezed her nipple.

Annie clutched her thighs together, searching for some relief. Her panties were soaked. It wouldn't take but a few strokes to make her come. She started to slide her hand into her pants.

"Having fun?" asked a deep voice from behind her.

She spun around, her heart dropping into her stomach. "Ah...I was just finishing cleaning in here." Damn, she should've closed the door but she hadn't expected anyone in this area. The rooms were off limits on this floor until tonight and she was the only one assigned to clean here.

He shut the door and locked it before strolling toward her. She'd seen him around the Club, but more than that she remembered him from the military photos her brother, Vic, had sent to her. She carried one of the three of them—Vic, Ethan and this guy, Patrick—in her purse. He'd been attractive in the picture, but now that he was older and in person he was gorgeous. He had dark green eyes, brown hair and a perfect body. He stopped so close to her his chest almost brushed against her breasts. She was pretty sure it would if she inhaled deeply. She really wanted to take that deep breath and feel his hard chest against her breasts.

"Don't let me stop you from enjoying the show."

"I…I wasn't. I should go." She started to walk past him but he grabbed her hand.

His grip was warm and strong but loose enough that she could pull free if she wanted. She didn't. Even though she only knew him from her brother's pictures and letters, she'd had many fantasies about him when she'd been in high school. Her gaze dropped to the front of his pants and her mouth almost watered. He was definitely interested. She dragged her eyes up his body, stopping on his face. He smiled at her.

"There's nothing to be embarrassed about. Watching turns us all on." He kissed the back of her hand and she jumped as his tongue darted out, tasting her skin.

"I…I should go." She didn't move.

"No, you should watch." He dropped her hand and grabbed her shoulders, gently turning her toward the mirror. He trailed his hands up and down her arms. "Watch."

The man in the other room was now sucking on the woman's breast as his fingers caressed her pussy.

"Would you like to hear them? Or do you like it quiet?" His voice was a rough whisper against her ear.

"Sound, please." She wanted to hear their gasps and moans. She wanted to close her eyes and pretend it was her. She shifted, squeezing her thighs together.

He chuckled as he moved away. She felt his absence to her bones. He'd been strong and warm behind her and for a moment she'd felt safe, safer than she had since her brother had come back from the war, broken and sad, and her father had started drinking again.

The woman's moans filled the room and Patrick came back to stand behind her, this time placing his hands on her waist.

"I'm Patrick," he said against her ear.

She couldn't take her eyes from the scene in front of her. The woman was almost coming as the man thrust his fingers inside of her.

"What's your name?" He nipped her neck and she jumped.

"I...I..." If she told him her name, he might say something to Ethan. Ethan would kill her if he knew she was in here watching.

"Tell me your name." His lips trailed along her neck and she tipped her head giving him better access.

The guy was kissing his way down the woman's body. Annie wanted to touch herself, to make herself come but Patrick was here.

He nibbled her ear. "Why won't you tell me your name?"

"I...I'll get in trouble." She rubbed her ass against his erection, hopefully giving him a hint.

"Tease." His hand drifted down her stomach, stopping right above where she wanted him to touch. "Tell me your name or I'll make you suffer." He unbuttoned her pants and left his hand—warm, rough but immobile—resting on her abdomen.

"I can't." She stood on tip-toe, hoping his hand would lower a little but he was too tall or she was too short. He had to be almost six foot and she was barely five-foot four. "I could get fired and I need this job."

"Darling, Ethan won't fire you for fucking a customer."

"We can't." She spun around. She hadn't thought this through. He was her fantasy come to life and she wanted him to be hers just for a moment, but Ethan would find out and then she'd be in deep shit.

"Don't worry. I'm a member and you work here, so we're both clean." He hesitated, his hands tightening on her hips. "Are you protected?"

"What?" She had no idea what he was talking about.

"Ethan makes sure everyone at the Club is clean but only the...some of his employees are required to be on birth control." He ran his hands up her sides, getting closer and closer to her breasts. "Are you on birth control?" His eyes darkened as they dropped to her tits. "If not, it's okay. There are other things we can do."

146

Oh, she wanted to do everything his eyes promised, but she couldn't. "No, I'll get in trouble. I need this job. I have to go." She tried to move but her feet refused to obey, so she just stared at his handsome face.

"Are you sure?" He bent so he was almost eye level with her. "I promise. Ethan won't care. A lot of maids become...change jobs. The pay's a lot better." His eyes roamed over her frame. "Especially, for someone as cute as you."

Ethan would kill her before letting her become one of his pleasure associates.

"I could talk to Ethan for you." His hands moved up her body, stopping right below her breasts.

Her nipples hardened and she forgot everything but what he was making her feel. He ran his thumb over one of them and she leaned closer, wanting him to do it again.

He did. He continued rubbing her nipple as he spoke. "I could persuade him to let me...handle your initiation into club life."

Her heart raced in her chest. It could be just her and him doing all these things she'd seen. Her pussy throbbed but she couldn't do it. She wouldn't do it. She couldn't have sex for money. Her parents were both dead but they'd never understand and she couldn't disappoint them. "No. I can't do that...not for money." Her eyes darted to the door. She needed to get out of there before she did something she'd regret.

"That's even better." He smiled as he stepped closer. "We can keep this between us. No money. Only a man and a woman." He leaned down and whispered in her ear, "Giving each other pleasure. A lot of pleasure. In ways you haven't even imagined."

There were moans from the other room and she glanced over her shoulder. The man's face was buried between the woman's thighs.

Patrick turned her around, pulling her against him and wrapping his arms around her waist. "Are you wet?"

"What? No." She struggled in his arms, her ass brushing against his erection again.

"Oh fuck. Do that again." He kissed her neck, open mouthed and hot.

She stopped trying to get away. She wanted this…this moment. She shouldn't but she did, so she wiggled her butt against him again. He was hard and long and her body ached for him. It'd been too long she'd had sex. She needed this.

"Would you like me to touch you?" His hands drifted over her hips and down her thighs.

She'd like him to do all sorts of things to her. She nodded.

"Say it." His words were a command she couldn't disobey.

"Yes."

"Yes, what?" He untucked her shirt from her pants.

"Touch me. Please." She was already pushing her hips toward his hand. She wanted his hand on her, his fingers inside of her.

148

"Are you wet?" he asked again.

She inhaled sharply as he unzipped her pants.

"Don't lie to me. I'll find out in a minute."

She'd never talked dirty during sex and she wasn't sure she was ready to do that with a stranger. Her heart skipped a beat. Maybe, she shouldn't be doing any of this with a stranger. She grabbed his hand. "Maybe, we shouldn't."

The woman below cried out and the man straightened, wiping his face and unbuttoning his pants.

"Watch. The main event is about to happen." Patrick's hot breath tickled her neck.

Her gaze locked on the man's penis. It was large and demanding. He straddled the woman, grabbing his cock.

"Don't you want to feel some of what they feel?" He nibbled on her ear and then neck. "I can help you."

She may not know him, but she trusted him. He was a former marine. He'd been a good friend of Vic's. He wouldn't hurt her and she needed to come. She loosened her grip, letting go of his hand. He slipped inside her pants, caressing her pussy through her underwear. His fingers were long and strong. She closed her eyes, leaning against him as he stroked her.

"You're already so wet and hot." His breath was a warm caress on her ear. "But, I'm going to make you wetter and then, I'm going to make you come." His other hand shoved her pants down, giving him more room to work. "Open your eyes and watch the show."

She did as he said. The man was inside the woman, thrusting hard and fast. The woman was moaning and trying to move but the restraints kept her mostly helpless.

"Fuck, you're soaked." Patrick's hand cupped her and she arched into his touch, rubbing her ass against his erection. He shoved his hand inside her underwear, his finger running along her folds until he slipped one inside.

"Oh." She grabbed his hand—not to push him away, but to make sure he didn't leave.

He smiled against her hair. "Don't worry, baby. I won't stop." He stroked his finger inside of her and his wrist brushed against her clit.

She needed more. She needed to touch him, feel him. She turned her head, wrapping her arms up and around his neck. He kissed her. It was desperate and wild, but he stopped too soon.

"They're almost done. You don't want to miss it."

She turned back to the mirror. The man below continued to fuck the woman as Patrick finger-fucked her. His other hand slipped under her shirt to her breast. His lips sucked her neck as he rocked his erection against her ass. He was everywhere, and she was so close. The muscles in her legs constricted. Her hips tipped upward.

"Wait, baby," he groaned in her ear, as he pushed a second finger inside of her. "Just a few more minutes."

His fingers were stretching her and it felt wonderful. She moaned, long and low as he thrust harder and faster, almost matching the pace of the man in the other room. She could almost imagine it was Patrick's cock and not his fingers inside of her.

"Oh...oh," she cried out. He was pushing her toward the edge. Her body was spiraling with each pump of his fingers. She was going to come—right here while watching that couple. It was so dirty and so wrong and it only made her hotter.

The woman below screamed and her body stiffened. The man thrust again and again and then grunted his release.

"Show's over." Patrick nipped her neck at the same time he pressed down on her clit with his thumb, sending her shooting into her orgasm.

She trembled and he pulled her close, his hand still cupping her pussy and his fingers still inside of her. When her heartbeat had settled, he removed his hand and bent, pulling off her shoes and removing her pants before lifting her and carrying her to the wall.

"My turn." He wrapped her legs around his waist.

Her phone rang. "My work phone. I...I have to answer it."

"When we're done." He unzipped his pants.

"Annie, answer the phone. I know you're around here. I can hear it ringing you stupid bitch," yelled Julie.

"Oh, shit." She shoved Patrick away, and ran across the room, grabbing her clothes off the floor. "It's my boss. She'll kill me if she finds me like this."

"I'll take care of Julie." He headed for the door, zipping up his fly. "Don't move." He grinned over his shoulder at her. "You can take off your pants again, but other than that, don't move."

"No. Please." She raced over to him, grabbing his arm. "I need this job." And Ethan could not find out about this.

"She won't fire you. She can't. Only Ethan can fire you." He bent and kissed her.

His lips were gentle and coaxing this time and her body swayed into him. He pulled her even closer and she could feel his cock, thick and heavy, pushing against her. Her pussy tightened again in anticipation.

"Damn it, Annie. This is going to be so much worse if I have to call your stupid phone again. Get out here!" Julie was only a few doors down.

She grabbed Patrick and tugged on his hand. "Please, hide." She glanced around, looking for somewhere that would conceal a six-foot muscular man.

"I'm not going to hide from Julie."

Get Your FREE Copy and find out what happens next

HTTP://MYBOOK.TO/VOYEUR_BK1

BOOKS BY ELLIS O. DAY
WWW.ELLISODAY.COM

LA PETITE MORT CLUB INTIMATE ENCOUNTER SERIES
YOU KNOW THE PLAYERS, BUT DO YOU KNOW THE KINK?

HIS LESSON (TERRY AND MAGGIE)
PLAYING HOUSE (NICK AND SARAH)
HIS IMPERFECT DAY (TERRY AND MAGGIE)

LA PETITE MORT CLUB SERIES

THE VOYEUR SERIES
THE VOYEUR **(FREE EBOOK)**
WATCHING THE VOYEUR (BOOK 2)
TOUCHING THE VOYEUR (BOOK 3)
LOVING THE VOYEUR (BOOK 4)

THE VOYEUR SERIES (BOOKS 1-4)

SIX NIGHTS OF SIN SERIES
Six Nights of Sin -The Complete Series: Books 1-6

INTERVIEWING FOR HER LOVER (BOOK 1) **(FREE)**
TAKING CONTROL (BOOK 2)

SCHOOL FANTASY (BOOK 3)
MASTER-SLAVE FANTASY (BOOK 4)
PUNISHMENT FANTASY (BOOK 5)
THE PROPOSITION (BOOK 6)

**SIX WEEKS OF SEDUCTION
A MERRY MASQUERADE FOR CHRISTMAS**

COMING SOON:

ETHAN'S STORY

MERRY MISTLETOE

MATTIE'S STORY

JAKE'S STORY

REBECCA AND DEREK'S STORY

VIC'S STORY

Email me with questions, concerns or to let me know what you thought of the book. I love hearing from readers.

authorellisoday@gmail.com

https://www.EllisODay.com

Follow me

Facebook
https://www.facebook.com/EllisODayRomanceAuthor/

Closed FB Group (sneak peeks, sample chapters, and other bonuses)
https://www.facebook.com/groups/153238782143373

Bookbub
https://www.bookbub.com/authors/ellis-o-day

Amazon
https://www.amazon.com/Ellis-O-Day/e/B072QL6B3G/ref=dp_byline_cont_ebooks_1

Instagram
https://www.instagram.com/authorellisoday/

Twitter
https://twitter.com/ellis_o_day

ABOUT THE AUTHOR

Ellis O. Day loves reading and writing about love and sex. She believes that although the two don't have to go together, it's best when they do (both in life and in fantasy).

www.ingramcontent.com/pod-product-compliance
Lightning Source LLC
Chambersburg PA
CBHW070553180626
46817CB00005B/1818